Betsy Ross

Designer of Our Flag

Illustrated by Al Fiorentino

Betsy Ross

Designer of Our Flag

by Ann Weil

Aladdin Paperbacks

Aladdin Paperbacks
An imprint of Simon & Schuster
Children's Publishing Division
1230 Avenue of the Americas
New York, NY 10020

First Aladdin Paperbacks edition, 1986
Printed in the United States of America

20 19 18 17 16 15 14 13

Library of Congress Cataloging-in-Publication Data

Weil, Ann, 1908–
Betsy Ross, designer of our flag.

Reprint of the ed.: Indianapolis : Bobbs-Merrill, c1983.
Published 1954 under title: Betsy Ross, girl of old Philadelphia.
Summary: Recreates the childhood of the woman traditionally remembered as the maker of the first American flag, which was secretly presented to General George Washington in Philadelphia in 1776.
1. Ross, Betsy, 1752–1836—Childhood and youth—Juvenile literature. 2. Revolutionists—United States—Biography—Juvenile literature. [1. Ross, Betsy, 1752–1836. 2. United States—History—Revolution, 1775–1783—Biography. 3. Flags—United States] I. Fiorentino, Al, ill. II. Title.

E302.6.R77W45 1986 973.3'092'4 [B] [92] 86-10775
ISBN 0-02-042120-6

To

Susan and Jill

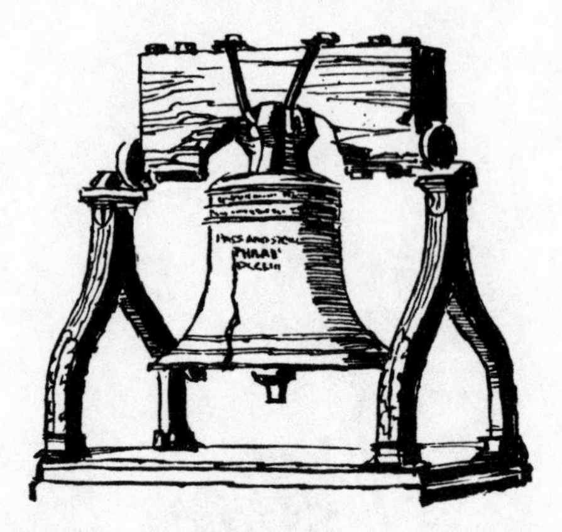

Illustrations

Full pages

Contents

★ ★

Books by Ann Weil

BETSY ROSS: DESIGNER OF OUR FLAG
FRANKLIN ROOSEVELT: BOY OF THE FOUR FREEDOMS
JOHN PHILIP SOUSA: MARCHING BOY
JOHN QUINCY ADAMS: BOY PATRIOT

★ ★ Betsy Ross

Designer of Our Flag

The Choice

Betsy Griscom looked thoughtfully up and down the long table. Her father and mother, her six older sisters, her small brother George, as well as Betsy herself, were sitting around it. Only Martha, two, and the baby, six months old, were already in bed. Betsy counted carefully.

"Ten people," she said, puzzled. "Ten people are sitting at this table, and there isn't room for any more. What are we going to do when the baby and Martha are old enough to sit with us at the table? Where will we put them?"

"We can always find room for all our children, Betsy," said Mr. Griscom, smiling.

"I am glad thee is a carpenter, Father," said George. "Thee is the best in all Philadelphia. Thee can build us a new table or anything else that we need to have."

"Father doesn't make furniture," said Sarah, who was twelve. "Fathers builds buildings."

"Thee could make furniture, too, if thee wanted to, couldn't thee, Father?" George was sure his father could do anything.

Mr. Griscom laughed. "I suppose I will have to make a new table whether I want to or not," he said. "Betsy is right. We are about to outgrow this one. I'll certainly have to make the new one before 1758 is over."

"Good," Betsy said, pleased. "We'll have the new table some time this year."

"I'll help thee, Father." George sat up very straight. He was only five years old, but since he was the only boy in the family he considered himself very important.

"I'll help thee, too, Father." Betsy raised her shoulders as high as she could. She was a year older than George. If he could help, she could help, too.

"Thee can't make furniture," George exclaimed. "Thee is a girl, and thee is too little."

Betsy didn't know what to say to George. It was difficult for a little girl to feel as useful as a boy. She looked at her plate.

"I can make doll furniture," she said. "I can make other furniture, too."

"Doll furniture!" George laughed. "Doll furniture doesn't count." He felt very grown-up. He forgot that he sometimes played with Betsy's dolls and her other toys.

"Doll furniture does count!" Betsy glanced at her mother. "It does, doesn't it, Mother?"

"Of course it counts." Mrs. Griscom smiled at Betsy. "Small things are often more difficult to make than large ones."

"Little girls come in different sizes, too," said her father, smiling at his seven daughters. "Don't worry, Betsy. Thee will soon grow up."

When dinner was over Betsy and George carried the dishes from the table to the kitchen. Then Rachel and Hannah swept the floor and straightened the room. Debby and Susan washed dishes. Mary and Sarah dried them.

"Let's go outside and play," suggested George when he and Betsy had finished their work.

"I can't." Betsy shook her head. "I want to make a table for my doll."

"Thee can't make a table. Thee is a girl and thee is too little," George said, laughing.

"I can make a table or anything else I want," Betsy said, stamping her foot. She ran out the back door and followed a narrow brick walk that led to her father's workshop. She tugged at the heavy door until she had it open. She stared at the tools hung on pegs around the room.

The tools looked heavy and unfamiliar. Betsy didn't know the names of most of them or how to use them. She was glad George hadn't come with her. She was sure he knew more about tools than she did. She didn't want her brother to remind her that girls didn't understand carpentry.

She walked around the neat, orderly workshop. She reached up to get a saw, but she could just touch the handle. By standing on some blocks of wood from a scrap pile she pushed up the saw so that the handle was free from the peg.

The big blade bent. The handle swung out and down. It hit Betsy on top of her head.

"Oh!" Betsy dropped the saw. It made a whining sound that seemed to say, "Thee is a girrl, a gi-rrr-lll, rrrr-llll."

Betsy rubbed her head. Then she laid the saw on her father's workbench. She wasn't going to let a bump on the head stop her. She intended to show George that she could make a table.

The scrap pile in the corner contained a real mixture of wood pieces. Betsy chose a few thin boards which looked almost the right length for her table. She liked the wood pile. She often played there with George on rainy days. While their father worked at his bench, the children built stores, houses, and schools. They built wagons and boats. They built tall towers that came tumbling down.

The woodpile was wonderful because it changed every day. Sometimes the pieces were short and thick. Sometimes they were all long and narrow. Today she could find both kinds.

Betsy placed a thin, flat piece of wood on the workbench. She lifted the saw and tried to put it against the wood just the way her father did. The saw was long and heavy. She could not hold the big, awkward tool with her right hand. It wobbled when she tried to saw through the wood. Betsy tugged and pulled.

Betsy wished she didn't have to make a table. It would be more fun to build a house out of all those wonderful pieces of wood before her father took them away. "But I have to build a table," she said to herself. "I have to show George that I can do anything he can."

Betsy put down the saw and rested for a moment. She knew that she would have to succeed in sawing the board. Again she picked up the saw and put it in place on the board. Then she tried to push and pull it, but had trouble holding it upright and keeping it straight. Its sharp teeth made little dents in the wood as they moved over the surface.

Betsy kept on trying. Finally the saw teeth began to give a little. Then—zing—and the saw jumped from the board to Betsy's finger.

"Oh!" She dropped the saw with an exclamation of pain. Again it seemed to say to her, "Theee is a gi-rrrr-llll. A gi-rrrr-llll."

Betsy rushed from the shop as soon as she saw her bleeding finger. She flew along the uneven brick walk until she reached the house. As she opened the door, she called to her mother.

"Look, Mother!" she cried. She held out her bleeding finger for her mother to see.

"Betsy! What happened, child?"

Betsy's eyes flashed. "Father's old saw bit me on the finger."

Mrs. Griscom looked as if she were swallowing a smile. She opened a cabinet drawer and took out a clean piece of old linen. She tore off a long, narrow strip and began to wrap it around Betsy's finger.

"Saw? Betsy, what was thee doing with a saw? Did thy father know thee was using a saw? Thee could get badly hurt."

"I was making a table for my doll."

"But, Betsy, thee does not know how to use a saw. Thy father's saws are very sharp."

"Thee said I could make doll furniture. Thee did. At dinner."

"I know I did, Betsy," said Mrs. Griscom, "but I did not think thee would try to use the saw. A saw is not for a little girl to play with."

Betsy hadn't cried when the saw hit her head. She hadn't even cried when her finger was cut. But when her mother said "little girl," the tears rolled down her cheeks.

"Every time I want to do something," she said, "I can't because I'm a girl, or because I'm too little. Little girls can't do anything!"

Mrs. Griscom tore the end of the bandage in half. She twisted it neatly and tied a knot. "Does thee really want to use a saw?" she asked.

Betsy looked surprised. "Of course I do," she said. "George says——"

"I'm not talking about George," Mrs. Griscom said firmly. "I'm talking about a little girl named Betsy. Does *she* want to use a saw?"

Betsy thought of the whining old saw that had hit her over the head and bitten her finger. Perhaps it wasn't so exciting after all. "Well——" she began.

Mrs. Griscom smiled. "Sit thee down for a minute," she said. "I will be right back."

Betsy wondered what her mother was going to do. She could hear her going down the hall and up the steps. She heard a drawer open and close. Then she heard her mother come down the stairs, through the hall again and back into the kitchen.

Mrs. Griscom walked across the room and sat down beside Betsy. "Hold up thy hands," she said, "and close thy eyes until I say 'Ready.' "

Betsy closed her eyes tightly. She felt something touch the first finger on her right hand.

"Ready!"

Betsy opened her eyes and stared. There on her finger was a beautiful silver thimble.

"Mother!" she cried. "Oh, Mother, it's beautiful! I want to use it right now."

Mrs. Griscom smiled. "My mother gave it to me when I was six years old," she said. "It was too large for me then, just as it is too large for thee now. But I grew into it, and so will thee. Now—" Mrs. Griscom held both of Betsy's hands up in front of her—"we have two hands and they are like two different people.

"The left hand," she went on, "is like a girl who is always trying to be someone else. This girl wants to be a boy, or she wants to be older, or she wants to be like someone down the street. She does things she doesn't like to do just because someone else does them. She never does them well and she is always getting into trouble.

"The right hand," Mrs. Griscom continued, "is like a different kind of girl. She doesn't waste time wishing for things that can never be. She is happy just being herself."

Mrs. Griscom looked at Betsy. "Which hand does thee like the better?" she asked.

Betsy looked at her left hand with the white bandage on the first finger. The ends of the knot stood up like little bunny ears that seemed to be wiggling at her. Having a bandage on her finger made her feel a little different and rather important. But underneath her finger hurt.

Betsy looked at her right hand with the thimble on the first finger. When she moved her finger back and forth the thimble swung to and fro like a little silver bell.

Betsy thought of all the times she had begged her mother to let her sew. Perhaps she was old enough now. She thought of all the things she wanted to make. Doll clothes were much more fun than doll furniture.

Betsy looked up at her mother and smiled. "I'll take the right hand," she said. "I *am* glad I'm me. I'll never try to be someone else again."

The Sour Dough

BAKING DAY! When Betsy woke the next morning, she could almost imagine that a delicious odor filled the house. But she was glad she couldn't smell the golden, crusty loaves baking. She intended to help her mother with this work.

Betsy dressed quickly and ran down the stairs to the kitchen. This was her favorite day of the week. It was the one day, too, when she was glad she was both little and a girl. Had she been older she would have gone off to school with her older sisters. And if she had been a boy, like George, she wouldn't have been able to help her mother with the baking.

George, too, liked to be in the kitchen on baking day. He watched Betsy as she climbed up on her stool beside her mother. He looked as if he would like to help knead the dough.

Mrs. Griscom had mixed the dough early in the morning. She and Betsy began to knead it after breakfast. They patted the dough into mounds. Then they stretched the dough, doubled it over into a mound again and pressed it with the palms of their hands.

George leaned against the kitchen table and watched them. He wished he could work with the dough, too. "Please." He moved a little closer to the kneading trough. "Please, may I help? I want a piece of dough, too."

Mrs. Griscom shook her head. "Baking is for girls. And boys, if they want to watch, shouldn't get in the way."

Betsy looked down at George from her high stool. Suddenly she was sorry for him.

He could have the workshop and all the tools. Baking was much more fun than sawing and hammering. She liked to feel the dough in her hands. It was soft and silky as a piece of cloth. She would have liked to bake every day.

They had almost finished when the baby began to cry. "Oh, dear." Mrs. Griscom hurried out of the room. "The dough is almost ready," she called back to Betsy. "Knead it a little longer and then put it to rise. And don't forget the sour dough," she added as she hurried up the stairs.

Betsy nodded to herself. She couldn't forget the sour dough. That was her favorite part of baking day.

When Mrs. Griscom mixed the dough for the week, she always put a little bit aside. Betsy knew that this was so that yeast could grow in the dough. This was very important—if they didn't have yeast, they wouldn't have bread. They'd have only dough that wouldn't rise.

Betsy always liked to hear her mother tell how she had brought a bit of sour dough from her mother's house to her new home after she was married. Betsy knew that her mother's mother had done the same thing.

"Just think," Betsy would say. "Week after week, year after year, a bit of dough has been saved. It links all the bread that thy family has made since they came to America."

No, Betsy couldn't forget the sour dough. She took out a handful, formed it into a little round ball and put it down on the table.

She gave the dough in the kneading trough one more pat and covered it carefully with a piece of white cloth. The wooden trough looked like a cradle. As Betsy tucked the cloth around it she felt as if she were putting a baby to bed.

"There." Betsy looked at George and smiled. "I can play with thee for a little while now. I can play until the dough has risen."

George was glad to play, but playing with Betsy on baking day wasn't very much fun. She kept running back to look at the dough.

"It will never rise if you keep uncovering it all the time," George said impatiently.

Betsy tossed her head. "Boys don't understand about baking," she said. "If it rises too much or too little the bread won't be good."

At last Betsy and her mother both agreed that the dough was just right. They spent the afternoon shaping it into huge loaves and baking them in the oven. Finally the last golden, crispy loaf was put on the big dining table to cool.

Betsy ran off to play with George again, and Mrs. Griscom began to put the kitchen in order. Finally the dishes were washed, the worktable was scraped clean and the floor was swept.

"Betsy!" Mrs. Griscom went to the kitchen door and called across the yard. "Betsy, where did thee put the sour dough? I'm ready to put it in the cellar."

"It's on the table!" Betsy shouted. "Right beside the kneading trough!"

"I can't find it, Betsy," Mrs. Griscom called. "I've looked everywhere."

Betsy stopped in the middle of a hopping race with George and ran toward the house. "It's right there, Mother. I'm sure it is."

She ran into the kitchen, climbed on her stool, and looked down at the table where she had been working. The kneading trough was there, but the sour dough was nowhere to be seen.

Once more Mrs. Griscom looked all about the kitchen. Betsy, right behind her, looked everywhere, too. They opened cupboard doors. They looked on the floor, in the flour barrel and even in the wood box. They opened drawers and took out all of Mrs. Griscom's neatly folded towels.

Betsy found a corncob doll that had been missing for a week. Mrs. Griscom found a knife that had fallen between the oven and the worktable. Betsy discovered a loose stone in the hearth. But neither of them found the sour dough.

"Mother, I'm sure I took out a piece of dough and put it here on the table," Betsy said.

Mrs. Griscom smiled. "Sometimes we think so much about something we are sure we did it. Perhaps thee just thought thee took it out."

"But I did. I know I did." There were tears in Betsy's eyes now. "I remember taking it out and putting it right here on the table."

"Well, thee mustn't feel too bad about it." Mrs. Griscom put her arm around Betsy. "Mrs. Adams, next door, will be glad to give us a bit of sour dough the next time she bakes. We won't be lacking in bread."

"But Mrs. Adams' bread isn't nearly so good as ours." The tears rolled down Betsy's cheeks. "Our bread will never taste the same now."

"Why, Betsy! Mrs. Adams bakes very good bread. Anyway, thee knows there is more to good bread than the sour dough. There's the mixing and the kneading and the rising. Thee knows how important they are."

"But that dough belonged to thee—and thy mother—and thy mother's mother." Betsy looked at the freshly baked loaves of bread on the table. "The bread won't ever seem the same."

Mrs. Griscom nodded. "It is nice to think of all the bread reaching so far back," she said. "I've often thought of all the hundreds and hundreds of loaves that have risen from that one bit of yeast my grandmother made when she was a young girl! But thee mustn't cry about it, Betsy. It isn't that important."

"But it is! It is!" Betsy felt as if something very precious had been lost—something no one could ever replace.

A few minutes later Betsy sat up and wiped her eyes. "But, Mother," she said again, "I'm sure I took the dough out. It has to be here in the kitchen. It couldn't have walked away. There was just thee and me and George——"

Betsy remembered that when George was smaller he always begged his mother for a piece of dough. He would knead it and work it and roll it into a ball. The longer he worked the smaller and dirtier it became.

He could never understand why his mother wouldn't bake his bit of dough with the rest of the bread. "It looks fine to me," he always said, looking with pride at the gray ball in his hands.

Now that George was five he felt too old to beg for some dough. But if he had happened to find a piece on the floor——

Betsy ran out of the kitchen and down the path. She knew they wouldn't be able to use the dough if George had been playing with it, but she had to know. "George!" she called. "George, come here a minute."

George hurried toward her.

Betsy looked at him sternly. "George, did thee find a piece of dough on the kitchen floor?"

"No." George looked puzzled.

"It was the sour dough," Betsy explained. "I took a piece out and now it's gone."

George shook his head. "I didn't see it," he said. "Honestly I didn't, Betsy."

Betsy walked slowly back to the kitchen. Was her mother right? Betsy still seemed to remember taking out the sour dough.

While she was looking over the kitchen again, her mother picked up the kneading trough. Betsy looked up as her mother passed.

"Mother!" Betsy sat down on the floor and put her head in her lap. "Mother, I——" Her shoulders began to shake.

At first Mrs. Griscom thought she was crying again. Then it sounded as if she were laughing. "Betsy!" Mrs. Griscom put the trough on the table again and knelt beside her. "What ails thee, child? What is the matter?"

"I . . . It . . ." Betsy gasped for breath. She couldn't go on.

"Mother," she said, "please pick up the kneading trough and look at the bottom of it."

Mrs. Griscom looked puzzled. "What is thee talking about?"

"Pick it up, Mother." Betsy whispered the words. "Then thee will know."

Mrs. Griscom stood up and lifted the trough off the table. Then, still puzzled, she looked down at Betsy.

"Look!" Betsy pointed to the bottom.

Mrs. Griscom raised the trough above her head. "Oh!" Now it was her turn to laugh. There on the bottom of the trough was something white. It was flat and smooth and looked like a new patch.

"Oh, dear." Mrs. Griscom shook her head. "I remember now that I moved the trough over a little bit when I was wiping the table. Of course it's so heavy it mashed the dough flat against the bottom of the pan."

Betsy and her mother smiled at each other. The Griscoms would still have bread linked to the hundreds of loaves of bread that had already been baked. The link wasn't broken after all.

Peppermint Stick Candy

Betsy rubbed her eyes. With a little cry she jumped out of bed. "It's here!" she cried. "It really is here. I didn't think it was ever going to come, but it's here. It's the day."

Betsy ran to the window and looked out. The day was certainly a nice day. It was a warm, sunny September morning in 1759. Below her, on the street, Betsy could see Mr. Grant, who owned the little grocery store on the corner.

"Mr. Grant! Mr. Grant!" She leaned far out on the window sill and waved her hand.

"Betsy!" Mr. Grant stopped, looked up at her and waved, too. "How are you today?"

"I am fine, thank thee. And I'm going to school. This is my first day."

"You don't say." Mr. Grant shook a finger at her. "Now, you be a good girl." Mr. Grant did not say "thee" and "thy" like her Quaker family. Mr. Grant was not a Quaker.

"I will."

"Stop by my store this morning," he said. "I might have a peppermint stick for a little girl on her first day at school."

"I will." Betsy laughed. "Thank thee, Mr. Grant. Thee is very kind."

"But you mustn't be late." Mr. Grant shook his finger at her again. "You'd better hurry."

"That's right." Betsy turned away from the window and walked across the room. Her new dress and bonnet were spread out on a chair waiting for her. The dress was gray and the bonnet was white. They looked exactly like her old ones, but they were new.

But Betsy didn't expect them to look different. They were Quaker clothes, and Quaker clothes always looked the same. These new clothes were exciting because they were new. Betsy was used to hand-me-downs from six older sisters. This was the first time she had had clothes made especially for her.

The first day of school, a new dress and bonnet, and a peppermint stick. Betsy was so excited she could scarcely dress. This morning, when her father left for work and the older girls left for school, she would be with them. She wouldn't have to stay home with George and Martha and the baby.

Betsy ran downstairs and into the kitchen. She helped herself to a large bowl of oatmeal and sat down at the table beside George.

"Wish I could go to school." George looked unhappy. "I wish I could go today. I'm tired of staying home while the rest go to school."

"It won't be long." Betsy felt very grown-up. She remembered when Rachel had said that to her. Now she was saying it to George.

"It will, too, be a long time." George blinked his eyes and tried to keep from crying. "It will be a whole year."

Betsy patted his arm. "I didn't think the day would ever come, either, but it did. It——"

"Hurry, Betsy! 'Tis late!"

Betsy looked up. Her sisters were ready to leave. "Oh, dear!" She finished her oatmeal quickly. "I have to go now, George. I don't want to be late the very first day."

As Betsy hurried down the walk with her older sisters she saw George standing at the window. His nose was pressed flat against the pane. He looked lonely and forlorn.

Betsy remembered how often she had stood at the window and watched the others go off. She felt very sorry for George.

"Good-by, George." Betsy walked backward and waved to him. "Good-by." She kept waving until they turned the corner. But even then she imagined she could still see his little flat-nosed face in the window.

When the girls got to the end of the street, Mr. Grant was waiting outside the store. He held out the peppermint stick and smiled at Betsy. "Here you are, young lady. A present for the first day at school."

"I thank thee very much." Betsy took the peppermint stick and looked at it fondly. She hadn't had one in a long, long time. Just smelling it was wonderful. She could already feel its tingly taste on her tongue. Just as she was ready to pop it into her mouth she thought of George's sad little face.

"Oh!" Without thinking and without a word to anyone Betsy turned around and started to run back home.

She went around the corner and up the path as fast as she could. George was still standing with his nose pressed against the window.

"Here." Betsy thrust the candy into his hand, turned around and ran out again. Down the path she went, around the corner and up the street. Then she stopped.

The corner was deserted. Mr. Grant was inside his store waiting on a customer. Her sisters had vanished.

"Oh dear!" Betsy looked around her. Could she find her way to school? She wasn't sure. Betsy knew the school was on Drinker's Alley. But where was Drinker's Alley? Should she turn right or left or go straight ahead? All the streets looked alike to her.

Betsy looked up and down the street. Then she began to turn around slowly, looking in every direction. Her sisters had gone on without her. She would surely be late.

Then, far in the distance, she saw six objects coming toward her. The six objects turned into six girls. The six girls turned into six sisters.

"Betsy!"

"Where has thee been?"

"What did thee do?"

"We lost thee."

"Where did thee go?"

"We didn't know thee wasn't with us."

Betsy looked from one sister to the other. But she didn't have a chance to answer any of them. Debby took one of her arms and Susan the other. They all began to run.

Betsy ran, too, but most of the time she was running in the air instead of on the ground. Debby and Susan were determined not to be late. They half carried her between them.

"There!" Debby and Susan put Betsy down in the schoolyard and hurried on with Mary and Sarah to their own school.

The four older girls no longer attended school on Drinker's Alley. They went to the Friends' School on South Fourth Street.

Now Rachel and Hannah were tugging at Betsy. "Come on," they said. "There's Miss Rebecca, ready to ring the bell. If we hurry, we won't be late."

Betsy looked around shyly at all the children in the schoolyard. Then, in a minute, her shyness disappeared. Miss Rebecca's school was a Quaker school and only Quaker children went there. Betsy had seen all of these children at meeting on First Day. They were her friends. "I see Abby," she said, "and Lucy and Ellen. I know all these girls."

They had reached the school steps and Miss Rebecca was standing at the top looking down at the children.

"Gracious, child," she said, looking straight at Betsy, "what happened to thee?"

For the first time Betsy realized that her bonnet was over one eye, her kerchief was turned backward, and her skirt was twisted to one side. She swallowed a giggle.

She wanted to tell Miss Rebecca that she had flown to school, but she thought that wouldn't be the thing to say. "I—" she began.

Fortunately Miss Rebecca had no time to wait for an answer to her question. "Oh dear," she said, " 'tis time for the bell," and she began to pull a long rope that hung just inside the door.

"Now go along." Miss Rebecca gave Betsy a little push toward the door. "And see that thee looks a little neater after this," she added.

Betsy wanted to say, "It was all because of the peppermint stick," but she knew Miss Rebecca wouldn't understand. She was sorry she didn't look tidy on her first day at school—but not too sorry. She was glad George had the peppermint stick to comfort him in his loneliness.

The Wagon Ride

THE GRISCOM family were coming home from meeting. Usually they walked two-by-two—Debby and Susan, Mary and Sarah, Hannah and Rachel, Betsy and George. Mrs. Griscom carried the baby, and Mr. Griscom carried Martha.

On this First Day, however, it was different. A young man named Edwin Bolton was walking with Debby. He walked home with her after meeting for two months. Then he began to call on her in the middle of the week. Before long he was having dinner with the Griscom family after meeting. Soon all the children thought of him as a member of the family.

Betsy was especially fond of Edwin. She always ran to meet him when he came. She always begged him to stay when he was ready to leave. She thought of him as a big brother.

Then, one day, Betsy ran up the stairs to George's room. George, who was playing on the floor, looked up and smiled. "Betsy," he began, "I wish thee would—"

"Sh!" Betsy put a finger to her lips. Then she closed the door quietly behind her.

George looked puzzled. "What's the matter, Betsy?" he whispered. "Why did thee do that?"

Betsy looked very serious. "George, I was walking through the hall just now, and I heard Mother and Father talking. Something terrible is going to happen."

"Something terrible?" George looked at Betsy. She did look pale. He began to feel frightened. "What's going to happen?" he asked. "Is someone ill?"

Betsy sat down beside George and folded her arms. "It's Edwin," she said. "Does thee know what Edwin is going to do? He's going to marry Debby and take her away. Debby isn't going to live with us any more. She's going to another house—with Edwin. We probably won't ever see her any more."

Debby? George looked puzzled. Debby was like a second mother to him. She had helped take care of him when he was little. He couldn't imagine their house without Debby. "Oh, Betsy," he said, shaking his head, "that is terrible. We can't get along without Debby."

"Well!" Betsy stood up and stamped her foot. "I've always liked Edwin. I thought he was nice. But if he's going to take Debby away——" Tears came to her eyes. "If he's going to take Debby away I'm never going to speak to him again, or go anywhere with him or . . . or anything! I want him to know how I feel."

George looked at Betsy. He remembered how Edwin had brought popcorn on cold winter evenings and helped them pop it in the fireplace. He had brought them peaches, too, from his father's farm. He had taken them for walks in the woods. In the summer he had shown them the places to find wild strawberries.

But if Edwin was taking Debby away—— George stamped his foot, too. "I won't either," he said. "I want him to know how I feel, too."

"When he comes this afternoon," Betsy said firmly, "I'm not even going downstairs."

George stomped around the room. "I'm not either," he declared.

A few minutes later Betsy and George heard the front door open. Then a deep voice called out, "Good afternoon, everyone!"

"It's Edwin." Betsy closed her lips tight. "Let's be real quiet," she whispered. "If he doesn't hear anyone maybe he'll go away."

But suddenly the house was filled with voices. Everyone had come into the living room to talk to Edwin. Betsy could hear her father's voice above the others. She couldn't tell what he was saying, but he sounded pleased and happy.

"Humph." Betsy tossed her head. "They can talk to him if they want to," she said. "I'm not going down."

"I'm not either." George shook his head, but he looked a little doubtful. It was always fun when Edwin came to the house. And he wondered why everyone sounded so excited.

At that moment the door to his room opened and Hannah looked in. "Come on downstairs," she said. "Edwin has brought his father's wagon. He's taking us all for a ride. Even Mother and Father are going."

George looked at Betsy. He had never ridden in a wagon. He knew she hadn't either. "Let's go, Betsy——" he began.

But Betsy was staring straight ahead as if she couldn't see either George or Hannah. "We're not going," she said.

"Not going?" Hannah stared at her in surprise. "Betsy Griscom," she said, "whatever is the matter? Why isn't thee going?"

"Nothing." Betsy tossed her head. "But George and I aren't going."

Hannah disappeared, but a few minutes later she was back again. "I don't know why the two of thee are acting like this," she said, "but Mother says she won't go unless both of thee go, too. She won't leave thee home alone."

Betsy looked at George and George looked at Betsy. "Well—" Betsy didn't know what to do. She thought how hard her mother worked day after day. Her mother went to meeting on First Day and to market once a week. Outside of that she seldom left the house. Her whole life was spent caring for her family.

Although Betsy didn't want to see Edwin, she knew that she couldn't keep her mother from going on this ride to the country.

"All right," she said. "We'll go, won't we, George? Mother won't have to stay home."

"Of course." George had wanted to go from the very beginning. He raced down the stairs two steps at a time.

It was fun in the big wagon. Mr. and Mrs. Griscom and Edwin sat up in front on the high wooden seat. The rest of the family sat on the deep bed of hay which Edwin had spread in the bottom of the wagon. Everyone laughed and talked—everyone except Betsy.

Betsy liked riding in the big wagon. She liked feeling the cool wind blow through her hair. She liked seeing roads and houses she had never seen before. But every time she looked at Debby she felt like crying. "Debby can't leave us," she whispered to herself. "She just can't."

They drove for a long time. When the sun began to set they were far out in the country. Then Edwin called back over his shoulder, "I'm going to show all of thee a house." He looked very pleased and happy. "It's the most special house in the world for me."

Everyone started to whisper and smile. They all seemed to know that this very special house was going to be Debby and Edwin's home after they were married.

Betsy looked at her older sisters. How could they be so happy when they knew Debby was going to leave them?

Betsy put her head down on her arm. Everyone thought she was asleep, so no one bothered her. Only she and George seemed to mind having Debby leave them.

But she wasn't asleep. She was thinking hard. And the more she thought about Debby's new home the more unhappy she became.

They had been driving all afternoon. That meant Debby and Edwin's house would be far away from their own house on Mulberry Street. "It will be much too far to walk," Betsy whispered to herself. "We'll be able to visit Debby only when Edwin can borrow his father's wagon." Betsy knew a busy farmer wouldn't be able to lend his wagon very often. "And the winters!" Betsy thought. "Sometimes the roads are so covered with snow, they can't be used for months and months. We'll never get to see Debby then. She could want us and need us, and we wouldn't even know it."

Betsy kept her head buried in her arms. She knew if she looked up she would begin to cry. Unhappy as she was, she didn't want to spoil the afternoon for everyone else.

They rode on and on. It seemed to Betsy they would never stop. But finally she heard Edwin's loud "Whoa!" and raised her head.

It was almost dark and Betsy couldn't see much. But even in the dim light she could see that they weren't in the country anymore.

Betsy blinked and looked about her carefully. She had never been outside Philadelphia before. She wanted to see everything in this strange town so far away from home.

She blinked again. There seemed to be something familiar about this street. The houses looked like houses she had seen before. She began to wonder if all towns looked the same as Philadelphia.

Then she saw little Janey Adams walking down the street. Janey lived next door to the Griscoms', not in a strange city. Janey would be in Philadelphia and she would surely be on Mulberry Street.

It *was* Mulberry Street! Suddenly all the houses looked familiar. Debby looked down the street and saw her own home.

"Everyone out!" Edwin jumped down and held out his hands. One by one, the Griscoms jumped out of the wagon.

"Well, here it is." Edwin looked at Debby and smiled. "Does thee like it?"

Everyone looked at the house except Betsy. She looked down the street at their own house not far away.

"You see," Edwin went on, "I thought it would be nice for Debby to be close to all of thee. If we live here thee can come to visit her as often as thee like."

Betsy still hadn't looked at the house, but she ran up to Edwin and grabbed his arm. "Oh, Edwin," she cried, "I think it's the most beautiful house in all the world."

Everyone laughed, and suddenly Betsy felt very happy. Debby was going to be close to them after all. And Edwin would be her brother-in-law! "Almost like George," Betsy said to herself.

Betsy went up to her brother. "I suppose," she whispered, "we do need a few more boys in the Griscom family."

George looked around at his nine sisters. "I'll say we do," he said. "I hadn't thought of it that way." Then he looked at Betsy and smiled. "Did thee like the wagon ride?" he asked.

"I didn't like it," she said softly, "but I do now. Oh, George." She laughed. "I think it was a wonderful ride."

By the time Betsy's eighth birthday had passed, Edwin and Debby were married and living in their own house down the street. And everyone was very happy about it—especially Betsy and George.

The Visit

"BETSY, can thee see anything?"

"No, George. 'Tis dark as pitch in there. I can't see a thing."

"I can't either. Betsy, does thee think he is in there? The whole place looks empty."

Betsy and George stood on tiptoe. Their noses were pressed hard against a window. Above their heads was an old sign with the words "Benj. FRANKLIN, Printer & Bookshop."

"Well!" Betsy turned away from the window. She put on her bonnet and began to tie the strings under her chin. "It's no use, George. We might as well go home. We can't see a thing."

"But I did so want to see him. Let's wait a little while longer, Betsy. Perhaps he is here, and he'll come out soon."

The children's interest had been aroused the evening before, when Edwin had mentioned meeting Dr. Franklin at the printing shop. This famous man often had pamphlets printed there, although he no longer ran the business. Betsy and George had listened in amazement while their father and Edwin had discussed some of the accomplishments of Benjamin Franklin.

Besides publishing an almanac and a newspaper, he had raised the money to establish a hospital and a school in Philadelphia. He had improved the postal system and the fire department. He had founded a circulating library. He had made a lightning rod that kept buildings from being damaged by lightning.

Dr. Franklin had recently returned to Philadelphia from England, where he had succeeded in getting laws passed which were favorable to the colonies. He had been honored by several European countries for his scientific writings.

Suddenly the children heard a pleasant voice. "Good afternoon!"

"Oh " Betsy and George were frightened by the unexpected greeting. They both jumped back, startled. "Oh!"

"You wanted something?" The tone was low and friendly. There was a smile on the man's round face.

Betsy and George looked at each other. They had wanted, more than anything else, a little glimpse of Dr. Franklin. Now that they saw him face to face they didn't know what to say.

"Oh!" Betsy felt that it was up to her to say something. "Well . . ." She stopped again. How could she tell a famous man that she and George just wanted to look at him for a few minutes? Her face grew red.

Dr. Franklin seemed to guess what she was thinking. He opened the door a little wider. He motioned for them to come in.

One minute Betsy and George were on the street in the bright sunlight. The next minute they found themselves inside the printing shop.

It was cool and damp inside. There was the unfamiliar smell of ink. Betsy looked around curiously. She had never been inside a printing shop before.

"This is very nice. I like having visitors." Dr. Franklin pulled two high stools. "Sit down and tell me about yourselves." He looked over his spectacles at Betsy. "First, now, tell me your names."

Betsy folded her hands on her lap. She sat up very straight. She looked as if she were answering a question in school. "My name is Elizabeth Griscom," she said, "but everyone calls me Betsy. This is my brother George."

"Griscom?" Dr. Franklin repeated the name. "Could you be Samuel Griscom's children?"

"Yes, sir. We are."

"The Griscom family settled in Philadelphia a long time ago," said Dr. Franklin.

Betsy looked pleased. "Yes, sir, they did. My great-grandfather came to America in 1681. He was here even before Mr. William Penn came over from England."

"My, that was a long time ago. Quakers like your great-grandfather helped William Penn found Philadelphia and make it such an important city," said Dr. Franklin.

"It's the largest city in America, too, isn't it?" asked George. "And I think it's the finest city in America."

"Yes, it's the largest city in the colonies," said Dr. Franklin. "And we are still trying to make it the finest city in America, the kind of city William Penn dreamed about."

"I always want to live in Philadelphia," said Betsy. "Exciting things happen here."

"Philadelphia is my favorite city, too," said Dr. Franklin. "I'm glad to be home again after spending a long time in Europe."

"I'd rather live in the colonies than in any city in Europe," Betsy said.

"You're a dyed-in-the wool American, Betsy," said Dr. Franklin, bending down and looking at her closely. "Now let's see if I can guess how old you are. I'd say you're about ten."

"That's right," Betsy smiled. "I was born on the first day of the week, the first day of the month, and the first day of the year, in 1752."

At that moment the big bell which hung in the State House belfry began to ring and its deep, low tones filled the room. The type rattled. The windows clattered. Even the pewter cups on the shelf danced up and down in time to its ringing. Betsy began to laugh. "I know something else that happened in 1752," she said. "That was the year the big bell in the State House came over from England."

"That's right." Dr. Franklin smiled at her. "I had forgotten that. I was there on the wharf the day it arrived. I even followed it all the way up the street to the State House lawn."

"I followed it, too!"

"Weren't you rather young then?"

"Yes." Betsy laughed. "You see, Father helped build the State House belfry. So the whole family was excited when the big bell finally came. I was just a baby, but Mother took me anyway. She held me up high so I could see it. She says everyone was pleased when the first note rang out. It was so clear and loud. But then the second note——"

Dr. Franklin nodded. "I'll never forget that second note," he said. "It was so dull and flat we couldn't believe our ears. We couldn't believe our eyes, either The very first note had made a great crack down one side."

"I would have sent it right back to England to be recast," said George.

"That is what a great many people wanted to do," Dr. Franklin answered. "But the captain refused to take it back. You know, the bell weighs two thousand pounds. He said he wouldn't have room for it and his new cargo. And we were in a hurry to have the bell.

"Finally a foundry near Philadelphia said they would try to recast it," Dr. Franklin went on. "They took the old bell and made a mold. Then they broke the bell into small pieces and melted them. After that they poured the metal back into the mold."

"Was it a good bell?" George looked up. "Did it have a good sound?"

Dr. Franklin shook his head. "It was a terrible bell. It sounded as bad as the old one after it was cracked. It went *bung! bung! bung!* It sounded as if someone was pounding on a big, old kettle. People put their hands over their ears every time it rang."

George laughed. It was funny to think of all the people in Philadelphia standing with their hands over their heads every time the bell rang. "It doesn't sound like that now," he said. "What happened?"

"The foundry decided to try again," Dr. Franklin answered. "You see, this was the first large bell ever made in America. All of us wanted to be proud of it. But it is very difficult to learn how to make a good bell. It was a long time before they found the right recipe."

"The right recipe?" Betsy laughed. "Do they need a recipe to make a bell?"

"Of course they need a recipe to make a bell," Dr. Franklin said. "Bell metal is made of copper and tin and bronze. They have to use just the right amount of each to get a strong bell with a good tone. They had to guess at the amounts."

He looked at Betsy. "If you used two cups of baking powder and one teaspoon of flour you wouldn't have good biscuits, would you?"

Betsy threw back her head and laughed. "They'd rise so high in the oven they'd pop the door wide open," she said.

Dr. Franklin nodded. "Well, that's the way it is with bells—they need to be made of exact amounts of ingredients. The bellmakers tried so much of this and so much of that and a little bit of the other."

He looked at Betsy again. "Does your mother ever bake one cooky first before she bakes the whole batch, just to see if the recipe is right?"

"Oh, yes." Betsy nodded. "She always does."

"Well," Dr. Franklin went on, "that's what the bellmakers did. They made little bells and tried them until they got the right tone."

Betsy and George looked at each other and laughed. It was funny to think of men making little bells and then ringing them to see if they were right.

"I wish I'd been there," said Betsy.

"I do, too," George said.

"I do, too," said Dr. Franklin. "It must have been a big day when they finally made one that was just right. Then, you see, they took that same recipe and cast the bell again. This time the tone was good. And so far," he added, smiling, "it hasn't cracked. Now tell me this! Do you know what is written on the bell?"

"Oh, yes." Betsy didn't hesitate for a minute. "It says: 'Proclaim liberty throughout all the land unto all the inhabitants thereof.' It's from the Bible," she added.

"Why that's fine. I'm glad you know what it says." Dr. Franklin looked pleased. "I wonder how many people listen when it rings."

He was silent for a moment. "It was good to hear the bell ring again when I came back from England," he continued. "Every time I hear it ring it seems to say, 'Liberty! Liberty!' That's what the people wanted it to say."

Dr. Franklin looked out the shop window for a few minutes. "Philadelphia is full of bells," he said. "Some say, 'Come to church.' Some say, 'Time for work.' Some say, 'Hurry to school.' The big bell on the rocks out in the harbor cries, 'Danger!' The night watchman's bell says, 'All is well!' Some bells cry, 'Fire!' Some bells strike the hour. The market bells say, 'Come and buy.'

"But my favorite bell is the State House bell. It says, 'Liberty!' every time it rings. It is right that here in America its voice should be louder than all the other bells put together."

He looked at Betsy and his eyes twinkled. "I'm glad you and the 'Liberty' bell are twins. It's a nice kind of twin to have."

Betsy felt happy. How nice of Dr. Franklin to have called the bell her twin!

Betsy could have stayed there all afternoon talking to Dr. Franklin. But she knew she shouldn't stay too long. "We must go now," she said, slipping off the high stool. "Thee has been very kind, Dr. Franklin. Thank thee very much for a pleasant afternoon. George and I will never forget this visit with thee."

Dr. Franklin walked to the door with them and waved as they hurried off.

It wasn't far from Dr. Franklin's printing shop on Second and Race streets to the Griscom house on Mulberry Street. Betsy and George ran all the way.

"I do hope Mother won't think we were rude," said Betsy, running even faster. "And I hope I'm not too late. This was my night to help cook supper. I have to make the pudding. Edwin and Debby are coming over, too."

"And I have to get water from the well and fill the wood box," said George.

Finally they were home. They hurried up the steps and lifted the latch. All the members of the family were busy at their own work.

Betsy hurried to the kitchen. Without a word she took down a large, white apron and tied it around her waist. George grabbed the water bucket and started for the well.

They both knew there would be no time to talk until all the chores were finished. Their story of the afternoon's visit would have to wait.

Betsy didn't mind waiting. She was rather glad she could keep this bit of news as her own secret for a little while. It seemed to make it last longer. And that was very important.

Betsy's visit with Dr. Franklin had seemed like a real adventure to her. She didn't know when anything half so exciting would ever happen to her again.

"Waste not, want not," was the household motto. Everything had to be used sparingly and carefully—food, clothing, water, wood—even a story. Betsy knew that this one small adventure would last for many a long winter evening.

The New School

When Betsy was ten she felt very grown-up. She was too old for Miss Rebecca's school. Now she could go to the Friends' School on South Fourth Street.

Betsy had been very eager to go to this large public grammar school. She had counted the months, the weeks, and the days. She was going to school now with her older sisters.

When they reached the schoolyard Betsy's sisters ran off to see their old friends. They were so excited about being back in school, they forgot that this was Betsy's first day. She stood there alone, feeling friendless and forlorn.

Betsy looked at the boys and girls who hurried past her. Many of them weren't Quakers. They were different from her old friends and very grown-up. Everything was different. Betsy had thought the big school would be exciting. Instead she felt lonely and very small. Tears came to her eyes and rolled down her cheeks.

At that moment Betsy's oldest sister, Sarah, came back to look for her. "Betsy Griscom," she said, "why is thee crying? What ails thee, child? Thee was eager to come to school."

"I don't like it here." Betsy brushed the tears from her eyes. "I wish I could go back to Miss Rebecca's school. I want my old friends. They're like us. They're all Quakers."

"Fie!" Sarah took her little sister's hand. "Thee will make new friends fast enough. After all, this is a Quaker school. Boys and girls who aren't Quakers come here from all over Philadelphia. Some of them are very wealthy."

"They could go anywhere, but they chose this school," said Mary, who had also remembered her little sister. "Isn't thee glad the Quakers run such a good school?"

Betsy nodded her head. "But they seem so different," she said. "So grown-up."

Sarah laughed. "Thee will grow up, too, Betsy. It will not take long."

Sarah was right. Betsy did grow up fast during that year. Before long she had made many new friends. She soon found that it didn't make any difference at all whether they were Quakers.

And her friends found out in no time that Betsy was as gay and friendly as she was pretty. Her white Quaker bonnet didn't hide her bright-blue eyes or her curly hair.

School started at eight o'clock in the morning. For two hours there were reading and writing and arithmetic. Then the teacher would tap on his desk with a ruler.

"Ten o'clock," he would say. "Now it is time for each pupil to work at that art or trade she most delights in."

"Most delights in." Betsy always repeated these words to herself. They were wonderful words. Betsy knew very well what art or trade she most delighted in. There was no doubt about it. Betsy Griscom "most delighted in" sewing—and now she could sew.

For two wonderful hours every morning Betsy sat with her head bent over her work. Why were the two hours from eight to ten so long? Why were the next two hours so short?

At twelve o'clock all the pupils went home to eat. Then at two they were back in school again. Once more, from two until four, there were reading, writing, and arithmetic. At four the ruler tapped again. Once more there were those wonderful words: "Now each pupil may practice that art or trade she most delights in."

And once more, for two wonderful hours, Betsy could work on her sewing. Then at six o'clock it was time to go home.

One evening Betsy and her friend Susannah Claypoole were walking home from school. It was late in December and quite dark at six o'clock. At the corner of the street the lamplighter was at work.

Susannah kicked a rock with the toe of her shoe. "I'm tired of school," she said. "Aren't you, Betsy? It's dark when we leave home in the mornings. It's dark when we come home in the evenings. We even have to go on Saturday mornings. We never have time to do anything else. I want to have some fun."

Betsy looked down at the big carpetbag she was carrying. "Oh, I don't mind!" she said. "The time seems to pass quickly. I almost finished my quilt today. I already know the pattern for the one I'm going to make next."

"Oh, you!" Susannah laughed. "As long as you can sew you don't care about anything else. Don't you ever get tired of sewing, Betsy? Don't you ever want to knit or weave for a change? I have almost all the mittens knitted for the family to wear this winter."

Betsy shook her head. "I like to sew best," she said. "I'm going to make shirts for George and Father before long."

"I suppose you like to sew because you sew so well," Susannah went on.

"Or maybe I sew well because I like it," Betsy answered. "I like to make fine stitches."

Susannah stopped in the middle of the sidewalk. "I never thought of that before. Do we do things well because we like to do them, or do we like to do them because we do them well? I like to knit and I do it well."

Betsy laughed. "I don't know. Perhaps 'tis a little bit of each."

Susannah looked at Betsy. "Anyway, you're lucky. You're lucky because you like to do what you do well, and you do well what you like to do. You're lucky, too, because you're pretty. Everyone says you're the prettiest girl in school."

Betsy's cheeks turned red. "Oh, that isn't true!" she cried. "Thee is pretty, too. Thee should be very glad thee is thee."

Susannah laughed. "I am glad I'm me. And I'm glad you're you. But most of all I'm glad we're friends."

"I am, too." Betsy smiled. "Thee is my very best friend, Susannah. I'm so glad we go to the same school."

Something Exciting

BETSY enjoyed school, but she also liked the long summer months. "Isn't it wonderful?" she said as she and Susannah walked down the street together. "No lessons for three whole months! We can have so much fun."

"What shall we do?" said Susannah. "Let's do something special to celebrate our vacation."

"I know," Betsy said. "Let's go down to the wharf. I like to look at the ships. Perhaps a ship from England has come in."

Susannah wrinkled her nose. "You always want to go to the wharf. I'd like to go somewhere else for a change."

"But 'tis so exciting down there," Betsy said. "Something's always happening. It's not the same place really, because it changes every day. There are always new boats and new people and new cargoes."

"And new smells." Susannah wrinkled her nose again.

"Oh, I like the smells," Betsy said. "I like the smell of tar and turpentine and paint and spices."

"All right, I'll go with you this time. But I'll tell you right now, I'm not going down to that wharf every day. So there!"

"Oh, I wouldn't want thee to." Betsy pretended to be shocked. "I wouldn't think of going more than every *other* day."

"Not every other day either." Susannah laughed in spite of herself. "I don't know why I always give in to you, Betsy. I suppose I'll end up spending half the summer down there with you. But I'd rather walk in the woods."

Susannah was silent for a minute, looking at the sky. "It's going to rain. I really don't think we should go today."

"But this is the first day we've had even a tiny bit of sunshine for ever so long," Betsy said. "Let's go anyway." She untied her bonnet strings. " 'Tis warm and it wouldn't be too terrible if it did rain. I won't melt, Sue, and neither will thee."

Betsy looked up and sniffed the air. " 'Tis an exciting day, with the wind and the dark clouds and the sun breaking through. Perhaps something exciting will happen."

Susannah laughed. "You always think something exciting is going to happen but it never does. Don't you know by now that nothing exciting ever happens to us?"

"But it could," Betsy said. "Exciting things happen to all kinds of people. This is our day, I feel sure, for something exciting to happen."

"And exciting things don't happen to a lot of people, too," said Susannah.

Betsy laughed. They had walked almost to the river. She could smell the water and hear the gentle lapping of the waves against the old gray wooden wharf.

"Sue!" Betsy grabbed Susannah's hand. "Look! We're in luck. There's a big ship in the harbor—a really big one—from England."

"How do you know it's from England?" Susannah asked. "You can see only the top of the mast from here."

"I can see the flag," Betsy said.

"Well, maybe you can tell what country a ship is from by its flag," said Susannah, "but I certainly can't."

"Susannah Claypoole!" Betsy stopped in the middle of the path and stared at Susannah. "Thee doesn't mean to tell me that all flags really look alike to thee."

"Oh, no, of course not," Susannah said. "I know they have different colors and different designs. But I don't know which flag belongs to which country."

Betsy laughed. "Each design means something. It tells something important that's happened to a country—something to remember. Why, a flag is like a page out of a history book, flying in the breeze."

They were close to the big ship now. Betsy and Susannah sat down on the wharf to watch. The gangplank had just been lowered. There was a great deal of noise and confusion. Sailors rushed back and forth shouting to one another. Passengers walked slowly as if they were afraid to walk on solid ground.

"They still have their sea legs," said Betsy, laughing. "They're so used to walking on the rolling deck, they don't know how to walk on flat ground any more."

The girls were too busy watching the ship to notice that someone was standing beside them.

"Good day!"

Betsy and Susannah looked up. A boy was standing beside Betsy. He took off his cap and smiled at them.

Betsy and Susannah looked down so their bonnets hid their faces. They weren't supposed to talk to strange boys. They pretended they hadn't seen him and looked the other way.

"Ahem!" The boy twirled his cap on the end of his finger. "Ahem!"

Betsy and Susannah looked up but they stared straight at the ship. As far as they were concerned the boy might have been a log on the wharf or a piece of rope.

He was certainly as quiet as a log or a piece of rope. Time and time again Betsy thought he had gone away. But when she tilted her bonnet and glanced to her right he was still there. Every

time she looked at him he smiled and twirled his cap. But Betsy always looked away quickly, as if she hadn't seen him.

Suddenly the sun disappeared. The clouds became darker and the wind stronger. Susannah looked up at the sky. "We'd best go," she said.

A sudden gust of wind swept up from the river. Before Betsy could grab her bonnet it had blown off her head and was skimming along toward the water.

"I'll get it." The boy scampered over ropes and around barrels piled on the wharf. He almost ran into sailors and passengers who had recently left the English ship. His coattails flew out behind him. By this time the bonnet had blown close to the river.

"He'll never catch it," Betsy said. "We might as well go home."

Then they saw the boy running toward them. He was twirling the bonnet over his head.

“ ’Twill be no good by the time he gets it here,” Betsy said. “It might as well have gone into the river as to be blown over the wharf.”

But the bonnet looked surprisingly fresh when the boy handed it to her a few minutes later.

“Thank thee.” Betsy reached for the bonnet. “Thank thee very much.”

“My name’s Joe Ashburn.” The boy held onto the bonnet strings. “I’ve seen you down here lots of times. You must like ships,” he said.

“She certainly does.” Susannah laughed. “I think she would live on a ship if she could.”

“Really?” Joe looked at Betsy and smiled. “I’m going to live on one someday,” he said. “My uncle owns three big ships. I’m going to sea on one of them just as soon as I finish school.”

Betsy forgot she wasn’t supposed to talk to strange boys. “I think I’d be a sailor, too, if I were a boy,” she said. “But girls can’t be sailors. I’ll probably never even get on a boat.”

"Haven't you ever been on a big ship?" Joe looked as if he couldn't believe her.

Betsy shook her head.

"Would you like to go on one?" he asked.

"Like to?" Betsy's eyes were sparkling. "Indeed I would."

"Right now?" Joe said. He nodded toward the river. "The captain of that big ship, who is a good friend of my uncle's, is going to be at our house for dinner tomorrow. I'm sure he'd let me take you aboard if I asked him. I've been on lots of other times the ship was in port."

"Oh, I couldn't," Betsy said, startled.

"Why not?" Joe looked puzzled.

"Sue and I couldn't go alone," she answered. "Our mothers wouldn't like it."

Joe laughed. "But you won't be alone," he said. "I'll be with you and——" He stopped. "But who are you? I must tell the captain your names when I talk with him."

"See," said Betsy, "thee does not even know our names. We couldn't possibly go with thee."

Joe laughed again. "That's no excuse. I imagine you could tell me your names if you tried real hard."

Betsy couldn't keep from smiling. "All right," she said. "My name is Betsy Griscom and this is Susannah Claypoole. But we don't know thee. We can't go with thee."

"Why not?" Joe asked again. "The ship will be here for weeks unloading and loading again. It isn't going to sail away with you aboard."

"Oh, I know that!" Betsy tossed her head. "It's just that—"

"Walking around up there will be just as safe as walking around here on the wharf," Joe said. "Nothing could happen to you. And I'll show you all over the ship," he went on eagerly. "I'll show you the guns, and how the sails work and everything. Come on. It'll be fun."

Joe pointed up to the deck. "Look! Wouldn't you like to stand 'way up there? The ship rocks back and forth. If you look down the river it's almost like being out on the ocean."

"Come on, Sue." Betsy tied the strings of her bonnet under her chin. "This may be the only chance we'll ever have to go on a big ship like that. I'll go if thee will."

Joe didn't wait for Susannah's answer. "You two stay here for a few minutes. I'll go up and talk to the captain. I won't be long."

He was off before the girls could say anything. They watched him as he ran across the wharf, down the steps and out toward the gangplank. When he got to the gangplank he stopped and looked from side to side. Suddenly he hid behind a stack of barrels.

He waited until several people, including two sailors, went on down the wharf. By that time the gangplank was clear.

"Well!" Susannah put her hands on her hips and pressed her lips together. "Now what do you think he's doing?" she asked. "That's a strange way to act, I must say!"

Betsy shook her head. "I can't imagine," she said slowly. "Why would he want to hide?"

As they watched they saw Joe peep out from behind one of the barrels and look from side to side. Then, quick as a lizard, he darted out from his hiding place and scurried up the gangplank.

Betsy and Susannah were too surprised to say anything. They began to walk slowly across the wharf, down the steps and out toward the ship. Their eyes were on Joe every minute.

"Look! He's hiding again!" Susannah pointed toward the deck.

Betsy shrugged her shoulders. Susannah was right. She could just see Joe's head sticking over the top of a large coil of rope. Then he disappeared again.

Betsy felt angry and disappointed and puzzled, but she couldn't keep from giggling. " 'Tis a queer way to visit the captain," she said.

"Captain, my eye!" Susannah said. "I don't think he knows the captain. I don't think the captain's coming to his house for dinner tomorrow. I don't think his uncle has three ships. He probably doesn't even have an uncle."

Betsy giggled again. It was all so silly. Still she was disappointed. It would have been fun to go on the ship and look around. "Why did he tell us all that if it wasn't true?" she asked.

"Boys!" said Susannah, as if that explained everything. "He thought you were pretty, Betsy Griscom, and he wanted you to think he was important. Next time he sees us down here he'll probably have some wonderful excuse and expect us to believe it."

Betsy nodded. "I suppose thee is right, Sue. We might as well go home."

As they turned and started to walk away, they heard someone running.

"Wait! Wait!" a voice behind them called.

They looked around. Joe was running toward them as fast as he could.

"Please wait just a minute for me," he shouted. "I have something to tell you."

The girls stopped. "I wonder what he's going to tell us this time," Susannah said.

"Whew!" Joe sat down on a rock and tried to catch his breath. "I thought you'd gone," he said, gasping. "I couldn't find you."

Susannah put her hands on her hips. "I don't know about you, Master Joe Ashburn, but we've no desire to hide behind barrels and coils of rope when we go aboard a ship."

"Oh, that!" Joe laughed. "You won't have to hide. I've got everything all arranged. You're invited to visit the ship right now."

"Then why did thee?" Betsy asked.

"Well, you see," Joe explained, "I don't know this crew. If I had told them I know the captain, they would have laughed at me. They would have thought I was just making it up. They would never have let me on the ship. So I had to sneak on when no one was looking."

Betsy and Susannah looked at each other. Was Joe really telling the truth? It was hard to know what to believe.

"Come on." Joe took each girl by the arm. "See the captain up there on the deck? Look, he sees us. He's waving."

The girls looked up at the deck of the ship. The man who stood there had so much gold braid on his uniform that they knew he had to be the captain. He seemed to be looking at them, and he was certainly smiling and waving.

"Come on." Joe led them toward the ship.

"The captain is a very busy man. He can see us in a few minutes."

A few minutes later they reached the top of the gangplank. The captain was talking with two of the ship's officers.

Joe was as good as his word. He took the girls from one end of the ship to the other. He told them the names of the different sails and how they were used. He took them up to the bridge and into the captain's quarters.

Finally he took them to the bow of the ship. "Now!" He looked at Betsy and smiled. "Close your eyes and take a deep breath."

The wind was rising higher every minute. Dark clouds raced across the sky. The sun appeared and then disappeared again. The big ship rolled from side to side. A few drops of rain began to fall.

The wind began to blow harder. The ship tossed and turned. The drizzle turned into a downpour. The gathering storm made their visit to the ship a much more exciting adventure.

Betsy opened her eyes wide and threw back her head. The wind blew through her hair and whipped at her skirts. She liked the feel of the wind and the rain on her face.

"It's like being in the middle of the ocean," she said. "I feel as if I'm sailing to England—to India—clear around the world. 'Tis the most exciting thing I've ever done."

Susannah ran for cover, and in a few minutes Betsy and Joe followed her.

Betsy tilted her head until she could see the flag at the very top of the ship. The wind had stretched it straight. There wasn't a fold or a ripple. "The flag looks as if it were pasted on the sky," she said. "It's so smooth and straight. And so bright," she added. "Look how it shines through the rain."

A moment later the captain came up to them. "I have a problem," he said. "Perhaps you would be willing to help me?"

"Yes, sir." Joe stood at attention. "I'll be glad to do anything I can."

"Mary Allen, a young girl from England, sailed on my ship with her maid," the captain explained. "Her parents died last year, and she has come to America to live with her uncle. He was supposed to meet Miss Allen here and take her back to his home in Baltimore.

"A few minutes ago I received a message from Mary's uncle. He left Baltimore three days ago, but heavy rains washed out the roads and he has been delayed. He asked me to take Mary to the inn and place her in the care of Mrs. Baker, the innkeeper's wife."

The captain frowned. "Everything has gone wrong," he said. "Mary's maid is ill and they should get to the inn as soon as possible. However, I can't leave the ship now—some very valuable cargo is being unloaded. I'd appreciate it if the three of you would see Mary and her maid to the inn. I'm sure if you go with her she will be in good hands."

The Sovereign

HALF an hour later a carriage stopped in front of the inn. Joe got out first, then he helped Betsy and Susannah. When Mary started to step out, the horses lurched. There was a loud ripping sound. Mary's full skirt had caught in one of the wheels. Her lovely dress, which had been so new and fresh, was muddied and torn.

"Oh, dear!" Mary tried to brush her torn, mud-splattered skirt. " 'Twas the last clean dress I had. We were on the ocean for two months. Water was very scarce and we couldn't wash our clothes. I saved this dress so I'd look nice when I met my uncle. Now look at it!"

"Oh, I'm so sorry, Miss Mary!" The maid leaned back against the carriage seat and closed her eyes. "Here I am ill and not able to do a thing to help you."

Betsy thought the maid looked even paler than when they had left the ship.

"Don't worry about that." Mary looked down at her dress. "You wouldn't be able to fix this anyway. It's too badly torn. I'll simply have to throw it away. It's ruined."

The dress did seem to be completely ruined, but Betsy looked at it carefully. "It can be fixed," she said finally. "I'll fix it for thee. Does thee have a needle, thread, and pins?"

"I don't see how you can mend it," Mary said. "Look, the whole side is torn."

Susannah patted Mary's arm. "If Betsy says she can fix it, she can. Don't you worry. She may be only twelve years old, but she can sew as well as her mother."

"Hush!" Betsy put her hand over Susannah's mouth and laughed. "Don't listen to her," she said. "But I can fix thy dress for thee. I'm sure I can make it look very good."

An hour later Mary was standing on top of a stool. Betsy walked slowly around her. She pinned tucks and straightened the hem until the front of Mary's dress looked like a pincushion.

"Now." Betsy picked up the needle and thread and thimble Mary had taken from her trunk. She began to take big stitches where the pins were. "Turn slowly, Mary. We'll soon have the dress as good as new."

Mary looked down at her gratefully. "This is almost like making a new dress," she said. "Really harder, because the material was torn. You're a wonderful seamstress, Betsy."

Betsy laughed. " 'Tis fun," she said. "Thy dress is beautiful, Mary. The material is lovely. It feels good in my hands."

Betsy worked on the dress all afternoon. She replaced the big stitches with tiny, even ones. Finally every ruffle and flounce was back in place. The tucks and the hem were straight again. The dried mud had been brushed off. It did, indeed, look like a new dress.

By late afternoon the storm had cleared and the sun was shining brightly. "Thy uncle will surely come soon," Betsy said as she told Mary good-by. "It won't take long for the roads to dry this time of the year. He'll be here soon."

"I hope so." Mary looked lonely standing at the inn door. "Will you come back in the morning?" she asked. "Even if he does come we won't leave right away. I want you to meet him."

Betsy was pleased by the invitation. She felt as if she and Mary were old friends. "I'll see thee tomorrow. I'll be here early."

"I wish Philadelphia was nearer to Baltimore," Mary said. "I'd like to see you often."

The next morning Mary, smiling happily, waited outside the inn. Betsy did not have to be told that Mary's uncle had arrived.

"He's here," Mary called as soon as Betsy was close enough to hear her. "He came in early this morning."

A tall man came to the doorway. Betsy almost gasped. "Mary's uncle must be a very rich man," she thought. Every curl of his white powdered wig was in place. He had silver buckles on his shoes and his purple coat was made of satin. His shirt had row upon row of ruffles. His cane had a golden head. "No wonder Mary wanted to look her best when she met him."

His smile was as friendly as Mary's. "Well! Well! I've been hearing a great deal about you, young lady. I don't know what my niece would have done without your help. I wanted to leave right away for Baltimore, but she wouldn't go without telling you good-by."

Betsy curtsied. "'Twas nothing," she said. "It was a pleasure to help her."

Mary's uncle looked toward a large carriage that was standing in the street. Betsy noticed that it was already loaded with Mary's baggage. The coachman held the reins in his hands. Mary's maid was already inside.

"Good-by." Mary held out both hands to Betsy. "Perhaps we'll meet again someday. And thank you again for all you did. I can never tell you how much it meant to me."

They stepped into the carriage. The footman closed the door. Then they were off.

Betsy stood still and watched the big carriage roll down the street. The girls waved handkerchiefs at each other until the carriage and the horses had disappeared around a bend.

Betsy started walking slowly down the street. But before she had gone very far, she heard someone calling to her.

"Wait, Miss Betsy! Wait!" Betsy saw the innkeeper running toward her and waving his hands. She stopped and waited for him. She couldn't imagine why Mr. Baker would want to talk to her.

"Miss Betsy!" Mr. Baker was puffing and panting when he stopped beside her. He was a fat man and not used to running. "Miss Betsy—" he tried to catch his breath—"the gentleman who was here with his niece left this with me."

He opened his hand and there in his palm lay four shillings and one sovereign. "Two of the shillings are for Miss Susannah," he said, "and the other two are for Master Joe."

He looked at Betsy and smiled. "The gentleman said the sovereign was for the little seamstress who was so kind to his niece."

Betsy stared at the money. It looked like a small treasure there in the innkeeper's hand. She couldn't believe her eyes.

"Oh, no," she said, "I couldn't take it!"

"But it's yours," Mr. Baker said. "It certainly isn't mine. Here." He opened Betsy's hand and put the money in it. "Now along with you. I can't stand here all day dilly-dallying and letting my dinner burn black in the oven. Just be glad you were blessed with nimble fingers."

Betsy didn't know whether to laugh or cry. She felt like doing a bit of each. A whole sovereign! That was a great deal of money. She closed her right hand tightly and put her left one over it. She had never had so much money in her hands before. She could hardly believe it. She felt like a very rich lady.

When Betsy was almost home she saw Susannah coming toward her down the street. "Sue!" Betsy had never been so glad to see her before. All the way home she had been bursting with her news. Now, at last, she could give Susannah her share and tell her the whole story.

Susannah's eyes grew round. She looked gratefully at her own two shillings. Then she looked unbelievingly at Betsy's sovereign. "Oh, Betsy," she cried, "isn't it wonderful!"

Betsy nodded. "I still can't quite believe it," she said. "And won't Joe be surprised? Come on, Sue. I'll run home and tell Mother about the sovereign and put it away. Then thee and I will find Joe and give him his share."

Susannah smiled. "Oh, Betsy," she said, "you were right. Something exciting can happen to anyone." She threw back her head and laughed. "Even to us!"

Ice Skates In July

Betsy hurried down the street with her sovereign in her hand. Now, at last, she could buy something she had wanted for a long time.

Betsy knew she shouldn't run. Running wasn't proper for a young lady. Besides, it was a very hot day. But she walked faster and faster. Every minute seemed important.

"Skates!" Betsy said the word softly to herself. She was so excited she didn't realize she was talking aloud. "I've always wanted a pair of skates. But skates are expensive," she explained to herself. "I never expected to have a pair. But now I can have some of my very own."

Betsy turned the sovereign over in her pocket and closed her eyes. She could imagine herself gliding over the ice. "It will be wonderful," she whispered. "Just wonderful." She began to walk even faster.

"Only one more corner." Betsy took off her bonnet and fanned herself. Hurrying along the street in the July sun had made her very warm. She was glad Mr. William's blacksmith shop wasn't any farther.

"Mr. Williams! Mr. Williams!" Betsy shouted. The blacksmith had his back turned toward the doorway. He was hammering on a piece of iron. "Mr. Williams, may I come in?"

"Come in! Come in!" Mr. Williams looked back over his shoulder. "Hello there, Betsy. I'll be through in a minute."

Betsy stepped into the shop and looked around. She was glad the blacksmith was busy. She wanted plenty of time to look at the skates.

Betsy walked around slowly. She had seen skates hanging on the walls of the shop many times. But there was none there now. There were horseshoes and harnesses and yokes. There were iron pots and skillets and candle molds. There were cranes and wheels and wagon tongues. There were big locks and keys.

But no skates! Had they all been sold?

At last the hammering stopped and Mr. Williams turned around. "Well, well," he said, wiping his hands on his leather apron. "This is a nice surprise. I've had only three customers so far today. They were all horses badly in need of shoes. 'Tis nice to have a charming customer for a change. What can I do for you?"

"I'm afraid, Mr. Williams, thee can't do anything. Thee does not have what I want."

Mr. Williams looked surprised. "I don't have what you want? I have everything a blacksmith shop should have. Everything!"

"Thee does not have skates."

"Skates?" Mr. Williams stared at Betsy. "Did you say skates?" he said very loudly.

Betsy felt as if she had asked for a stick of peppermint candy or a baby bonnet. She didn't know what to say.

"What ails you, child?" Mr. Williams asked.

Betsy shook her head. She felt more bewildered every moment. One did buy skates at a blacksmith shop. She was sure of it. Why did Mr. Williams look so surprised?

"Ho, ho! Skates! Skates!" Mr. Williams put his hands to his head and began to laugh.

Now Betsy felt provoked. "But thee does have skates, Mr. Williams," she said. "I've seen them here. I'm sure I have."

Mr. Williams looked at Betsy. "In July?" he asked. "You've seen skates here in July?"

"July?" Betsy stared at the blacksmith. Then she began to laugh, too.

"Oh, my!" he said. He wiped his forehead with his kerchief. "You want to buy skates on a day like this!"

"I didn't think," Betsy said. "I've wanted skates for a long time. Today, when I had the money, I thought about nothing else. I see now 'twas very foolish. I'd best go."

"Go?" Mr. Williams wiped his face again. "I thought you wanted a pair of skates."

"I did." Betsy looked around the shop again. "But thee hasn't any."

Mr. Williams smiled. "Well, I don't have a heap of customers asking for skates in July. But if you want them, you shall have them. I'll see what I have in the loft."

Betsy looked up at a small opening in the ceiling. "Oh, I wouldn't want thee to go up there, Mr. Williams. 'Twould be frightfully hot on a day like this. I can get the skates some other time."

Mr. Williams nodded. "'Twill be hot as four Julys. But I haven't had a good customer in three days. 'Twould be nice to hear a bit of silver tinkling in the drawer again."

He started up the narrow ladder. "Now, I'm not saying those skates won't be melted," he said as his head disappeared. "Hot enough to melt anything up here. Don't know why I bother to keep a fire in my forge."

By this time his feet, too, had disappeared. Betsy could hear him walking around above her head. She could hear him moving heavy objects and opening and closing chests.

At last Betsy saw a foot at the top of the ladder. Then another foot. Mr. Williams' face was redder than ever as he looked down at her, but he was smiling broadly. "These are mighty fine skates," he said. "They came all the way from England. You won't find a better pair of skates anywhere in the colonies."

Betsy looked at the blades. They glistened in the dark shop. "Oh, they're the most beautiful skates I've ever seen."

Suddenly Betsy felt frightened. "How much are they?" she asked.

Mr. Williams pulled at his chin. "Well, as I said, they're mighty fine skates. Don't know when I'll get another pair like them. The price is one sovereign and five shillings."

"Oh!" Betsy put the skates carefully on the counter. She should have known they'd be too expensive. She'd have to buy cheaper ones."

"On the other hand," Mr. Williams went on, "sometimes we sell winter things a mite cheaper in the summer to get them out of the way."

Betsy looked up hopefully.

"But then again I spent a mighty long time in the loft looking for these skates. My time's worth something. I could have finished those horseshoes by now. Time's money, I always say."

Betsy nodded. Mr. Williams had spent a great deal of time in the loft. Her hopes fell again.

The blacksmith continued: "However, sometimes skates get a mite rusty during the summer if no one keeps an eye on them. It's a good idea for me to sell them if I can."

Betsy picked up the skates. If they had been made of silver they couldn't have looked more beautiful. "If I had them," she said softly, "I'd make a bag for them and oil them every day."

Mr. Williams smiled. "Every day would be a mite often. Once a month would be about right. Let's say we make the price an even sovereign. You'll never do better than that."

An even sovereign! Betsy couldn't believe that she had heard correctly. The hot July sun and the heat from the forge made her feel a little dizzy. She thought she must be dreaming. She couldn't believe she really owned the best pair of skates in the colonies.

"One sovereign," Mr. Williams repeated. "What with summer and the rust and not having a good customer for three days. . . . Yes, I'll sell them for a sovereign."

Betsy opened her hand and put the sovereign on the counter. The skates were hers, really hers. She couldn't believe it.

Betsy could scarcely wait for winter. She had made a little bag for her skates. She oiled them every month as Mr. Williams had said. Now they shone even more brightly than when she had bought them.

Finally it began to grow cold. On the first day of December the river began to freeze. By the end of the week it was hard enough for skating. Betsy hurried down to the river.

The wind howled, but Betsy didn't mind. The snow blew in her face, but she didn't mind that either. The river was frozen and her skates she had wanted so long were on her feet.

Betsy skimmed across the ice. "It's like flying. It's like—— Oh!" Betsy bumped into a tall boy who was skating in front of her. "I'm sorry," she said, "but my skates! They go so fast! I'm not used to them. This is the first time I've worn them. I'll try to be more careful."

The boy smiled at Betsy. Her cheeks were red and her blue eyes were sparkling. Her curly hair was blowing around her bonnet. "I'm not sorry," he said. "You're Betsy Griscom, aren't you? I've heard a lot about you."

"How did thee know me?" asked Betsy.

The boy twirled around on his skates and then made a deep bow. "I'm John Ross," he said. "I'm a friend of Joe Ashburn. He's told me about you. He's even told me about your skates."

Betsy smiled. "I don't see Joe often, but I've been talking about these skates for months. I'm sure all my friends are tired of hearing me talk about skates and skating."

"I don't blame you." John looked down at the skates. "They're beautiful. Can you make a figure eight with them?"

Betsy laughed. "Gracious, no! I've been on skates only a few times in my whole life. I can't do anything except bump into people."

"Figure eights aren't hard." John Ross looked at Betsy and smiled. "I'll teach you. I'm sure it will be easy for you."

It was easy for Betsy to learn. By the end of the winter John Ross thought she was the best skater in Philadelphia. He thought she was the prettiest girl in Philadelphia, too.

Philadelphia Winter

In Philadelphia there was always a great deal of illness during the long winter months. When Betsy was fourteen, the winter was colder than usual. There seemed to be more serious illness than there had been for a number of years.

Within a short time it seemed as if half the people of Philadelphia became ill with colds and sore throats. Every week there were fewer people on the streets, in the shops and the stores. Every week there were fewer Friends at meeting.

Of Betsy's sisters, Susan, Mary, and Sarah went to help friends and relatives who were ill. Hannah, Rachel, and Betsy were the only older girls left at home. Then Hannah and Rachel came down with sore throats. Only Betsy and her mother were left to do everything around the house and take care of the sick.

Every day Betsy hurried home from school to help her mother. She helped with the cleaning and washing and cooking. She helped take care of the younger children. She helped nurse Hannah and Rachel. At night she dropped into bed, too tired to think.

One night Betsy woke to find her mother bending over her bed. Mrs. Griscom was holding a candle in one hand. She was shaking Betsy with the other hand. "Betsy! Betsy! Wake up! Wake up! Thy father is ill, too. He woke suddenly with a very high fever. We should have the doctor right away."

"All right, Mother," Betsy said, rubbing her eyes and struggling to wake up. "I'll go after the doctor right away."

"Come, child, get up." Mrs. Griscom spoke urgently. "I hate to send thee out on a cold night like this, but I'm afraid to wait until morning for the doctor. Thee must dress warmly."

"I'll be all right, Mother," Betsy said. She was now wide-awake. "Thee mustn't worry. I'll bring the doctor. He'll know what to do."

"There's no one to go but thee—I'm afraid to leave Father. Take George with thee for company. It's a long way, and there's no time to lose."

Betsy, now thoroughly alarmed, had jumped out of bed and was putting on her clothes. Her heart was beating faster and faster.

Her father was never ill. He was always up in the morning before anyone else. He was the last one in bed at night. She couldn't imagine her father ill in bed like Hannah and Rachel.

She rushed to George's room. "George! George! wake up! Father is ill!"

"I hear thee, Betsy," George said sleepily.

"George!" Betsy shook him. "George! Get up! We must get the doctor for Father."

Finally George opened his eyes. He listened. He tried to understand what Betsy was saying. He blinked. Then he sat up very straight. Now at last he was awake. Thoroughly alarmed, he began to scramble into his clothes.

A few minutes later Betsy and George were standing in the hallway with their mother. Mrs. Griscom tied shawls around their heads and pulled their scarves a little tighter. "It's bitter cold outside," she said. "I hate for thee to go. I don't like to have thee on the streets late at night. It's a long cold walk to Spruce Street." She turned to Betsy. "Thee is sure thee knows where the doctor lives? Thee won't get lost in the night?" she asked.

Betsy nodded. "I'll know the house when I see it. Don't worry, Mother. We'll find him. We'll bring him back as soon as we can."

They opened the front door. "Oh!" Betsy couldn't keep from gasping. The cold air cut against her face like a knife. Her cheeks stung. Tears came to her eyes. It was hard to see. It was hard to breathe.

The hard snow crunched beneath their feet. Everything looked strange and different. There were no streets or walks or yards—only snow and houses where everyone was sleeping.

Betsy had never been out so late before. The cold snowy night was exciting. Suddenly she felt wide awake. "Come on," she said again. "Let's run. Then we won't get cold."

Just then they saw the night watchman. It was a relief to meet someone at last on the silent, deserted streets.

"Nine o'clock," he called. "Nine o'clock and all is well."

"Nine o'clock!" Betsy laughed. "I thought it was the middle of the night. I can't believe it. Why, I thought it was at least twelve."

"I thought it was midnight, too," said George. He still looked half asleep. He was hurrying to keep up with Betsy. He was too cold and sleepy to say anything more.

As they passed the State House, Betsy looked up at the belfry. Through the archways she could make out the faint outlines of the bell. How beautiful it looked against the starry sky! Once more she could hear Dr. Franklin saying, "I'm glad you and the 'Liberty' bell are twins. It's a nice kind of twin to have."

On and on they ran. They went up one deserted street and down another. At last they came to Walnut Street and Betsy stopped suddenly. The doctor lived in this part of Philadelphia, she knew, but where was Spruce Street? Where was his house?

She looked up and down the street. No one was in sight. There was no one to ask the way. Were they lost?

Betsy closed her eyes. She tried to remember how the streets looked in the daylight with all the snow gone. She hadn't been in this vicinity recently and had never been here at night.

"We're on Walnut Street," she mumbled. "The doctor lives on Spruce Street."

Then she opened her eyes. "Spruce Street," she said, holding George's hand tighter. "I know where it is now. Come on, George. We aren't lost after all."

"Were we lost?" George looked at her in surprise. "I thought you knew how to get there."

She smiled at him. "Only for a minute," she said. "But it's all right now. I know the way."

Betsy and George hurried on. They hadn't been in this part of Philadelphia often. Betsy, however, knew her way on Spruce Street.

When they finally reached the doctor's house, they were glad to find that he was awake. Betsy started to tell him about her father.

"Come in. Come in," the doctor interrupted. "Not another word until you come in and warm yourselves by the fire. You look nearly frozen." He led them to the sitting room.

Betsy and George stumbled over to the fireplace and sank down gratefully on the settle. The doctor listened carefully as Betsy told him about her father. "Stay close by the fire while I harness the horses to the sleigh," he said. "It won't take long."

In a few minutes the doctor's wife came in with two large mugs. She handed one to Betsy and one to George. Hot milk! They thought nothing had ever tasted so good.

By the time they had finished the milk the doctor was in the driveway. "Up we go!" He helped them into the sleigh. "Giddap!" He cracked his whip. They went racing through the snowy streets.

The horses ran faster and faster. The sleigh skimmed over the snow. It seemed to Betsy that she and George had run for hours through the streets. Now, in a few minutes, they were home again. They were not even cold.

A little later Betsy saw the doctor coming down the hall. "I've given your father some medicine," he said. "He's resting much better now. I believe his fever will be down by morning. I'm sure he's going to be all right. But he will need careful nursing for a few days."

"Oh!" Betsy was so happy she could scarcely speak. She smiled up at the doctor. Suddenly her knees felt very weak.

The doctor took her arm. "You'd better go to bed yourself," he said. "You've had a hard evening. You don't want to be ill, too."

Betsy was glad to do as he said. She hurried to her room and began to undress.

She was just ready to climb into bed when she saw the night watchman coming down the street. When he got directly in front of their house he rang his bell. Then he called out in his high, clear voice, "Ten o'clock! Ten o'clock and all is well!"

Ten o'clock! Had it been only one hour since she and George left home? It seemed impossible that so much could have happened in one hour. She was wide-awake and happy.

Betsy stood at the window for a few minutes. She thought again of all that had happened. She felt as if she had been to the ends of the earth and back again. What a strange, unbelievable hour it had been! But if her father was all right, everything was all right.

"Ten o'clock," she repeated as she climbed into bed. "Ten o'clock and all is well."

The next day Betsy went from one task to another as fast as she could. There was so much to do. She and her mother didn't stop for a minute all day.

At five o'clock Betsy fixed trays for her father and Hannah and Rachel. Then she fed the two younger children and put them to bed. Finally Betsy, her mother, and George could eat.

Betsy put three plates on the table. She put on three knives and forks and spoons. She put on three mugs. Then she stared at the table.

How strange it looked! How bare! How lonesome! The big table looked as if it, too, missed all the family.

The week passed slowly for Betsy. Then, on the following Monday, Mary came back. Within a few days Sarah and Susan had returned. Each day Betsy saw Mr. Griscom, Hannah, and Rachel grow a little stronger.

Two weeks later every member of the Griscom family sat down at the table together. How wonderful it was to be together again!

After supper Betsy looked at the big stack of dirty dishes. "Oh, Mary," she cried, "look at them! Aren't they beautiful?"

"Beautiful?" Mary stared at the dishes. What was Betsy talking about? "What is beautiful, Betsy?" she asked.

"Why, the dirty dishes," said Betsy. "I think they're just beautiful."

The dirty dishes? Mary stared at her sister. Was she going to be ill, too? Was she ill already? Did she have chills and fever?

Betsy laughed at her sister's surprised look. "Eleven dirty plates," she said. "Eleven dirty mugs. Eleven dirty knives and forks and spoons. They're beautiful, Mary. It means the family is all together again. Oh, Mary, I missed all of thee so. I didn't think I'd ever enjoy washing a lot of dirty dishes, but tonight it seems wonderful. It means you're all home."

Mary laughed. "Thee silly," she said. "Thee silly, silly, silly! But it's wonderful to be back, too. I guess thee's right. Dirty dishes can be rather nice. Come on silly. I'll help thee."

The Contest

ONE evening in December Betsy was strangely silent. She was sitting in front of the large fireplace with Sarah, Mary, and Susan. All of them were busily sewing.

Usually Betsy kept everyone amused with her stories. Tonight she had nothing to say.

After half an hour of silence, Sarah looked up. "Betsy," she said, "doesn't thee feel well?"

Betsy bent her head lower over her sewing. "Of course I feel well," she said. "Why?"

Sarah shook her head. "I don't know. Usually thee is such a chatterbox. Thee has not said a word all evening."

"I feel very well," Betsy answered, but there was a quiver in her voice.

Sarah looked up. She saw that Betsy's eyes were filled with tears.

"Why, Betsy!" Sarah dropped her sewing. She ran to her sister's side. "Betsy, something *is* wrong. What is the matter with thee?"

"It's nothing." Betsy rubbed her eyes with the back of her hand. "Really 'tis nothing. I'm silly and foolish. I should be ashamed of myself. And I am." Suddenly she put her head on the arm of her chair and began to cry.

All three sisters were around her now. They asked a dozen questions. Betsy was always so cheerful. She never cried. What was wrong?

Betsy sat up. She wiped her eyes. "Oh, dear," she said, " 'tis really so silly! I'm ashamed. It's just——" Betsy almost started to cry again. "It's just that they are going to have a great fair at the High Street Market four months from now."

Betsy's three sisters looked at one another. A fair wasn't something to cry over! What had happened to their little sister?

"But Betsy!" Sarah clapped her hands together. "That's wonderful news. Fairs are such fun. We'll all go. 'Tis very exciting."

"At the fair," Betsy went on slowly, "they are going to have an exhibit of handiwork."

"But they always do!" Sarah was more puzzled than ever. One didn't cry about handiwork exhibits either.

Again Betsy went on. "There are going to be judges. They are going to give prizes for the three finest pieces of needlework."

"Why, Betsy, that's splendid." Susan's eyes were shining. "What a chance for thee! Thee has won every sewing contest they've had at school since thee has been there."

Betsy shook her head. "This isn't a school contest. This is for anyone in Philadelphia."

Mary laughed. "That shouldn't bother thee, Betsy. Thee will be fifteen next month and Mother says thee can sew better than she can. In fact, Mother says thee does finer needlework than anyone she knows. Thee has a good chance to win the contest. Why is thee crying?"

Betsy spoke slowly, as if she were explaining something to very small children. "Anyone in Philadelphia may enter," she said. "Thee knows as well as I do what things will be exhibited. There will be beautiful evening gowns. There will be lovely afternoon dresses. There will be handsome bonnets. There will be dainty clothes for babies. There will be handsome bedspreads and wonderful quilts.

Betsy paused and sighed. "What can I enter? We don't need more bedclothes just now. Shall I make a plain white bonnet? Shall I make a Quaker shirt with four straight seams? Shall I make a Quaker bodice?"

"But, Betsy, surely the judges will look at the sewing," Sarah said gently. "The designs or the patterns shouldn't be too important. After all, it is a sewing contest. It's the sewing they'll judge. They'll give first prize for the handiwork with fine, even stitches."

Susan smiled. "And no one can take smaller stitches than thee, Betsy—no one in all Philadelphia. I'm sure of that."

Betsy shook her head again. "A man from the market came to school this morning. He told us all about the exhibit. He said we should make something different. Something original. Something that would make people say, 'Oh, how lovely!' Other people can make beautiful things from bright silks and muslins. What can I make that anyone would call lovely?"

Betsy's three sisters were silent. They suspected she was right. What chance would plain Quaker things have in such a contest?

Betsy wiped her eyes again. "I know 'tis foolish for me to care. I know 'tis wrong and worldly. But I can't help it. I'd work as hard as anyone. I'm sure I would. But I haven't a chance. What could a Quaker girl make?"

Sarah looked around the big room. It was clean and neat. Each piece of furniture shone from hard use and hard rubbing. But there was no decoration of any kind. Everything seemed to be something useful.

Then Sarah's glance caught something hanging on the wall—a small sampler. Betsy had made it when she was six years old.

Here was something without a use. "Thee could make a sampler for the exhibit," Betsy.

"A sampler?" Betsy laughed. Was her sister serious? "Why, Sarah, samplers are made by little girls when they are just beginning to learn to sew. What chance would a sampler have in a contest like this?"

"Thee could make a special sampler—a different one—a large one—a beautiful one." Sarah's eyes had a faraway look. "Betsy, thee could make one of the most beautiful samplers that anybody has ever made."

Betsy laughed again. "I may sew nicely, and thee is very kind to say so. But I know I could never do that."

"Why not?" Sarah opened her eyes wide. "Why not, Betsy? Sometime someone somewhere has to make the most beautiful thing of its kind in all the world."

"Sometime. Somewhere. Someone." Betsy repeated the words slowly. Could the time be now? Could the place be Philadelphia? Could she be the person to make the most beautiful sampler in the world?

For a few minutes Betsy's eyes sparkled. Then she became solemn again. She began to feel that such a dream could never be real.

"I couldn't make a big, beautiful sampler," she said. "Thee knows I couldn't."

"But thee could, Betsy. Thee sews so well."

"Thee knows Father and Mother would think it was a great waste of good time and good material," said Betsy.

Once more the four girls were silent. Her sisters knew Betsy was right. A large, fancy sampler would be worldly and wasteful.

The big clock on the mantel ticked slowly. All thoughts were on the contest, but for a long time no one could think of anything to say.

At last Sarah asked, "What are the prizes, Betsy? Are they worth having?"

Betsy looked up from her sewing. "The first prize is five pounds, the second three pounds, the third one pound. But it isn't on account of the prize money that I want to take part."

Sarah's eyes flashed. "We'll just have to think of something," she said. "We'll just have to."

She looked at the sampler again. At the bottom Betsy had stitched in crooked little-girl stitches the words, "Never put off till tomorrow what you can do today."

"Betsy!" Sarah was so excited she jumped out of her chair and ran to her sister's side. "Betsy, I have another idea! Maybe it's a good one this time. If thee would use a quotation from the Bible on your sampler, Father and Mother might not object to it."

"Of course!" Susan cried. "It wouldn't be just a decoration then. The other day Father said that we should always keep the words of the Bible before our eyes."

"But Father didn't mean that literally," Mary said. "He didn't mean we should have our walls covered with words.

"He meant that we should never forget the wisdom of the Bible. We should always follow the teachings of the Bible."

"Surely we are more apt to follow the teachings if we are reminded of them," said Susan.

"A sampler would be a way to have the words of the Bible really before our eyes," said Sarah.

"Oh!" Betsy stared at her sister for a second. Then she threw her arms around Sarah's neck. "Oh, that's indeed a grand idea. A grand——" She stopped suddenly and looked very serious. "I just hope," she added slowly, "that Father thinks it is a grand idea, too."

The Quotation

THE next morning Betsy told her father about the contest. Then she told him about the girls' idea for a sampler with a Bible verse that she could enter in the exhibit.

When she had finished, Mr. Griscom looked very serious. "Thee knows, Betsy, that we Quakers believe we serve God best by leading quiet, simple lives. We do not believe in ornaments of any kind."

Betsy held her breath.

"Good words do not need decoration," Mr. Griscom went on slowly. "If they speak the truth, that is enough."

"Yes, Father," Betsy said, trying to hide her disappointment. She wanted to go away where she could cry quietly.

"However, I do not think it would be amiss if a quotation from the Bible were hung on the wall where all could see it," Mr. Griscom continued.

"Oh, Father!" cried Betsy.

"And if thee wishes to make a design with thy needle and thread I do not think that would be amiss either."

"Oh, thank thee, Father!" Betsy felt like jumping up and down, but she knew that would not be proper. She decided to curtsy instead. "Thank thee very much, Father," she repeated.

"Has thee chosen the quotation yet, Betsy?"

"No, Father," Betsy replied. "I must read the Bible some more before I choose my verse."

"Thee should have no trouble making a choice," Mr. Griscom said. "The Bible is filled with many wonderful thoughts."

Betsy sat down and opened the Bible. What quotation should she choose? The Bible was so big. There were so many books. Each book had so many chapters. Each chapter had so many verses. Her father had said it would not be hard to choose. She found it very hard.

Betsy turned the pages of the Bible slowly. The first book was Genesis. Many of the verses seemed right, but not exactly right.

The second book was Exodus. Betsy shook her head. She was sure if she looked long enough she would find a very special verse—one that was just right for her.

The third book was Leviticus. Leviticus! Suddenly she knew the verse she wanted, but she couldn't remember exactly where to find it. She skimmed the pages quickly through chapter twenty-four. She glanced through the verses of chapter twenty-five. Number ten—there it was. It was like finding an old friend.

"Proclaim liberty throughout all the land unto all the inhabitants thereof," she read slowly to herself. The words stood out from the page as if they were printed in different ink.

That was the verse she wanted. That was the verse for her sampler. The more Betsy thought about it the more excited she became.

Closing her eyes, she could see the sampler just as she wanted it to be. There would be a picture of the big bell in the center. Around the edge, just as on the bell itself, she would put the quotation. And just as it was on the bell, she would put the date, too: 1752—the year she was born and the year the bell was made.

Suddenly Betsy didn't care whether she won the prize or not. It was the sampler now, not the prize, that was important to her.

The Sampler

THE next evening the whole family were sitting around the big fireplace. Each of the Griscom girls was sewing. The wind whistled and howled outside. The fire burned brightly.

Such a bright fire needed a lot of wood. Before long the wood box was empty. George looked at it and made a face. He would have to fill it again.

"Brrrrr!" He shivered. He didn't want to leave the warm, cheerful fire. He put on his heavy coat and wrapped a big shawl around his head. Then he picked up the wood basket and went outside.

When he came back again he was smiling. "I'm glad I went to get the wood," he said. "It's a beautiful night—clear and cold. The stars and the moon are shining. 'Tis like the night we went for the doctor. Remember, Betsy?"

Betsy smiled. "Of course I remember. I remember how black the big belfry looked against the dark-blue sky, how bright the stars were, how the moon shone——"

Suddenly Betsy stopped. "George," she cried, "that's the way I'm going to make my sampler! I'll have the big bell ringing out in the night. I'll make a dark-blue sky filled with stars. The moon will shine on the bell so thee can read the words. They'll stand out in the moonlight like . . . like the stars."

The next day Betsy started to work on her sampler. First she combed the wool until it was smooth. Next she spun it into yarn. Then she dyed the yarn in various colors.

Finally she could weave the cloth. Weaving the cloth, however, was only the beginning. Designing the sampler took much more time.

Every evening Betsy sat near the hearth and made sketches with a piece of charcoal. Somehow the sketches never quite satisfied her. The belfry did not form the proper background. The bell was too big or too small. There were too many stars or not enough stars. The moonlight did not look the way she remembered it.

One evening Betsy at last drew a sketch that seemed almost perfect. This time the bell was the right size. There was just the right number of stars and just enough moonlight.

But the stars themselves weren't quite right yet. Betsy had drawn their six points all straight and even, but she thought they looked stiff and strange. She sketched them again.

"The bell seems to ring," she thought. "But the stars don't twinkle."

Although Betsy tried over and over again she couldn't get the stars to satisfy her.

"Spring will be here," she said, "before I've even started to embroider the sampler."

Mrs. Griscom looked down at Betsy's sketches. "Perhaps five-pointed stars would look more like real stars," she suggested.

Betsy soon found, however, that five-pointed stars were hard to make. No matter what she did she couldn't make all the points alike.

Finally Betsy took the sketches to her mother. "I've tried and tried," she said. "I just can't make a five-pointed star."

"A five-pointed star is easy," said her mother. "Let me show thee how to make one."

Mrs. Griscom cut a square from a small piece of cloth. She folded the square in half. Then she folded the lower half up at an angle. Next she folded the lower edge to the upper edge of

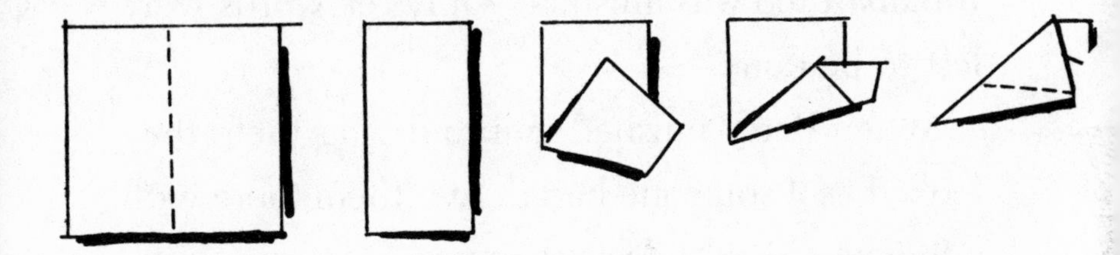

the fold. Then she folded the upper half down over the lower section at an angle. Snip! One small corner of the folded cloth fell into her lap. She handed the other piece to Betsy.

Betsy carefully unfolded the cloth. It was a perfect little five-pointed star.

"Oh, Mother," she cried, "it's wonderful! How did thee learn such a thing?"

Betsy embroidered the ground first, and after that, the sky. As soon as she had finished the clouds, the little five-pointed stars began to twinkle in the sky. Betsy liked working on the stars best of all. They were so small and delicate. They reminded her of jewels.

Then the big bell began to appear, bit by bit. Finally it too was finished. Only the words were left to be done.

When Betsy finished embroidering them they looked as if someone had drawn them there with a fine pen. But, fine as they were, they could be read easily. They stood out clear and strong on the big bell.

Now at last the sampler was finished!

Booths for The Fair

EVERY afternoon on her way home from school, Betsy stopped at the High Street Market to look at the work being done. It was a busy place now. There was always something new to see. Workmen rushed around. There were sawing and pounding and hammering. Platforms appeared, and booths sprang up, one after the other. There was excitement everywhere.

One day Hannah and Betsy stood beside the needlework booth. The workmen were putting on the finishing touches and it looked very grand. A number of other people wandered about, staring at the various booths.

"Just think, Betsy," said Hannah, "soon thy sampler will be hanging in that booth. Won't thee be proud?"

"But perhaps they won't hang it." Betsy looked very solemn.

"Won't hang it?" Hannah stared at her sister. "Why wouldn't they?"

"Thee knows they don't hang everything," Betsy answered. "They pick only the best. Perhaps they won't think my sampler is good enough to show at the fair."

"Fie!" Hannah tossed her head. "They'll put it right out in front. Wait and see."

But as they walked home Hannah was quiet. The Griscoms had all been so sure Betsy would win—everyone but Betsy. Was Betsy right? After all, it was a big exhibit. Most of the things were made by grown women. Hannah knew that her little sister would be extremely disappointed if her sampler was not exhibited.

It seemed to Betsy and her sisters that April would never end. The hammering and pounding at the High Street Market seemed louder now. The workmen worked faster. Big signs appeared on the fences and lampposts: "THE HIGH STREET FAIR—SPECIAL EXHIBITS—GRAND PRIZES—STARTING MAY THE FIRST."

On the first of May Betsy carried her sampler down to the needlework booth. She thought the booth looked larger than ever. The man standing inside looked large, too. Betsy felt especially small. She wished she had never thought of the exhibit. She wished her father had not allowed her to make a sampler for the fair.

"Yes, my little maid?" The man looked down at Betsy. "You wanted something?"

"I . . . I . . ." Betsy felt smaller and smaller. "I have a sampler here. 'Tis for the exhibit."

The man smiled. Betsy thought he was laughing at her. Her cheeks grew red.

Without glancing at the sampler the man picked it up and tossed it onto a shelf. Then he picked up a quill and a small piece of paper. "Name?" he asked.

Tears came to Betsy's eyes. She wanted to stamp her foot. She wanted to take her sampler and run home with it. It might not be worth hanging up, but the man had no right to throw it around like an old piece of cloth.

"Name?" The man looked at Betsy impatiently. "What's your name, young lady? Other people are waiting."

By this time a number of other exhibitors were standing in line. Betsy cleared her throat and blinked. She wouldn't let anyone see that she was angry and ready to cry.

When she finally spoke, her voice was loud and clear. "Betsy Griscom," she answered.

"Address?"

"Mulberry Street near Fourth."

The man pinned the paper on her sampler. "They're hanging the things tomorrow," he said. "If your sampler isn't hung you're supposed to come and get it that afternoon."

Betsy hurried home. By this time her cheeks were burning with embarrassment. She certainly didn't want to think about her sampler or about the exhibit. She didn't even want to think of the fair—not until tomorrow.

Today and Tomorrow

Betsy opened her eyes. She sat up in bed and blinked. "Hannah! Hannah! Wake up!" Betsy shook her sister. "Wake up! 'Tis tomorrow."

Hannah rubbed her eyes sleepily. "It can't be tomorrow. 'Tis today."

"Silly!" Betsy laughed. "Does thee not know that today is tomorrow?"

Hannah rubbed her eyes again. "I'm still half asleep," she said, "and I think thee is, too. Such a way to talk."

Betsy jumped out of bed. "Well, the man said to come back tomorrow. Get up, Hannah! Doesn't thee want to go to the fair?"

"The fair!" Hannah was out of bed in a second. "It's today, Betsy! Oh, isn't it exciting? Dear me, we must hurry. There's so much to do before we go."

By two o'clock in the afternoon all the housework was finished. Now Betsy and her sisters could get ready for the fair. George was excited, too. He even put on his best suit and slicked down his hair without being told. "Not ready yet?" he asked. "I'm going now. I'll meet thee at the needlework booth."

" 'Tis like First Day," said Rachel. "It seems strange to be putting on our best clothes this afternoon. Now let's hurry to the fair and see if Betsy's sampler got a prize."

As they got close to the fair Betsy walked slower and slower. She wanted to go to the needlework booth. But she certainly didn't want to ask the man for her sampler and see him smile as he handed it back to her.

Then she saw George pushing through the crowd toward her as fast as he could.

"Betsy! Betsy!" His coat was off. His collar was unbuttoned. His hair looked as if it had never been combed. "Betsy! Thee should see it!"

"George!" Betsy grabbed his arm. "Stop shouting! Stand still! What's the matter? What has happened to thee?"

" 'Tis there, Betsy. I saw it."

"What's where?"

George was breathing so hard he could scarcely talk. "I ran all the way. I've been to the needlework booth, Betsy. And thy sampler is hanging right out in front where everyone can see it."

Betsy forgot that she was supposed to act like a young lady. She took George's hand and began to run. Somehow they managed to make their way through the crowds. They edged toward the needlework booth.

They ran in and out among the people, between the booths and around the vendors. Finally they came to the front of the needlework booth. A large crowd was already there.

"Oh!" Betsy stared at the sampler as if she had never seen it before.

"Isn't it beautiful?" George looked first at the sampler and then at his sister. "It's the most beautiful thing in the whole exhibit."

Betsy looked around quickly. "Hush, George, someone might hear thee. The sampler does look nice and I'm glad I made it. But 'tis far from being the most beautiful piece."

"I think it is," George declared. "It seems as if a great many other people are looking at it and talking about it, too."

Betsy smiled at him. "Thee says that just because I'm thy sister."

"No, I do not." George looked very serious. "It is the most beautiful, no matter who made it."

"Thee is a boy," Betsy answered, "and boys don't know about such things. See that beautiful evening gown up there? It's elegant. I'm sure it will win first prize."

"Well, I'm a boy, all right,"George said flatly, "and I may not know about such things. But I know what I like and I know what I think is pretty. The sampler is the prettiest thing here. I heard other people say so, too."

"Hush!" Betsy cried. "People will hear thee."

"I don't care who hears me say it. I'm going to say it as loud as I please."

"Hush! Hush, please!" Betsy's cheeks were getting redder and redder. "Everyone is staring at thee."

"I don't care." George was shouting now.

Betsy tried to look serious, but the corners of her mouth refused to stay down. George looked so funny standing there talking about her sampler at the top of his voice.

"Here come our sisters," said Betsy soothingly. "We'll see what they think."

The girls all praised the sampler again and again. But they had to agree with Betsy that the evening gown would surely win first prize.

The afternoon passed quickly. There was so much to see and so much to do. They had to make every minute count.

When the State House bell began to ring, Betsy and her sisters and George were at the far end of the fairgrounds.

"Oh!" Betsy looked up startled. " 'Tis five o'clock already. That's when they're going to award the prizes at the needlework booth."

They tried to make their way through the crowd as quickly as possible. It seemed as if everyone in Philadelphia had come to the fair.

When they got twenty feet from the needlework booth the press of people was worse than it had been elsewhere.

"Oh dear!" Betsy stood on tiptoe and tried to look over the heads of the people. "We'll never get close enough to hear or even see. We should have come back much earlier."

"It's too late to do anything about it now," George said. He jumped up and down. When he jumped up he could catch a glimpse of the platform. When he was down he could tell them what he had seen.

"There's a table up there," he said. "Four men are sitting around it. Now one is getting up and walking to the center of the platform. He's talking but I can't make out what he's saying."

George continued to jump up and down. "The man has taken down that evening gown thee were admiring. He's holding it up for everyone to see. He's talking again.

"Now a lady's walking up on the stage. I guess she's the one who made the gown. Yes, she did. The man's handing her the prize."

"See?" Betsy looked at George and smiled. "Didn't we tell thee the gown would win? Boys just don't understand about such things."

"I still think thy sampler better than that fussy old dress," George said firmly. "Who'd want to wear it anyway? That skirt's so full a woman couldn't get into a carriage with it on."

He jumped up again. "Well, the lady's left the platform and the man's talking. Now he's taking down a big quilt."

Betsy nodded her head. She had noticed a particularly well-made quilt on display. If that was the one George was talking about, it certainly deserved the second prize.

Now the second lady was on the platform receiving her prize. Betsy stood on tiptoe but she couldn't see her. "Oh, dear." She settled back on her heels again. "I'll be glad when this is over! I've stretched my neck so much I'm sure it must be an inch longer."

"Betsy! Betsy!" George shouted.

Betsy stared at him. "I'm right beside thee. Thee doesn't have to yell."

"Oh, Betsy!" George whispered this time. "Thee should see what the man is doing now!"

Betsy stood on tiptoe again and caught a quick glimpse of the platform. Suddenly she covered her mouth with her hand and said softly, "Oh, it just can't be! It can't be true."

"But it is. It is!" George was shouting again. " 'Tis thy sampler. Thee has won third prize."

Betsy had never felt so frightened in her life. She looked at George and her sisters. "I can't go up there," she said. "I can't push through this big crowd of people with everyone staring at me. I can't go up on that platform all alone."

Suddenly she smiled. "I'll just pretend I'm not here. If none of us says anything no one will know the difference. I can get the prize tomorrow. They didn't say we had to be here. I——"

"Betsy Griscom!" Hannah shook her gently. "Of course thee is going up there. Such nonsense! Thee should be proud to go. It's a wonderful honor. They're waiting for thee."

Betsy never knew how she got through the crowd and onto the platform. She pretended she was walking with her eyes closed. Somehow she felt that if she didn't look at anyone, no one would look at her.

The man in the center of the platform smiled at Betsy. Then he congratulated her and handed her the prize.

Betsy looked down at the money in her hand. It wasn't one pound. It was five pounds!

Betsy looked up quickly. "Thee has made a mistake," she said. "The third prize was to be one pound. Thee has given me five!"

"Third prize?" The man looked at her, astonished. "You didn't win third prize," he said. "You won first prize."

"First prize?" Betsy couldn't believe it. "But those other prizes—the gown and the quilt. I thought—— We couldn't hear but——"

The man smiled at her. "The gown won third prize," he said, "and the quilt second. You see, we always save the best for the last. If you remember," he went on, "when we announced the contest we said that prizes were to be given for the most original pieces. We all thought that your sampler was perfectly made and the most unusual piece in the whole exhibit."

He pointed at the gown and the quilt. "They're beautiful, of course, but the gown was copied from a French fashion and the quilt is an English design. We like your sampler because it is an American design made from American materials. America must learn to develop her own arts. Your sampler is a good beginning."

Betsy curtsied. "Thank thee. Thank thee very much." She couldn't say more.

Once again Betsy found her way through the crowd. Finally she was standing beside George and her sisters. Without a word she opened her hand and showed them the gold pieces.

George was the first to understand what had happened. "Thee won first prize!" He began to laugh. "So boys don't know about such things. What a pity. And the four judges were men. I suppose men don't know about such things, either."

It was late when they finally started home. The moon was high in the sky and the stars were shining. As they passed the State House, Betsy looked up and smiled. The stars seemed close and friendly. They looked as if they were almost touching the big belfry. "They do look five-pointed." She laughed. "I'm glad I made them five-pointed on my sampler."

The Apprentices

Betsy and George were coming home after they had spent the evening skating. John Ross came with them. John seemed to appear with increasing frequency wherever Betsy was.

He told Betsy that he had recently become an apprentice in an upholstery shop.

"Webster's is the best upholstery establishment in Philadelphia," he said. "After I learn all I can there, I'll have my own shop."

"It sounds so exciting," Betsy said. "I wish girls could be apprentices."

"Girls are apprenticed at Webster's," he said. "I wish you were there, too."

John bade them good night and turned the corner toward Christ Church. Betsy stood outside for a moment looking at the stars. Her cheeks were pink with exercise and excitement, and her heart was beating fast.

What fun it would be to work at Webster's, she thought. She could see John and other interesting people every day. She was sure she would be able to learn the work. She could already sew unusually well.

She went into the house and sat down near the fireplace. Her father was moving about in the next room. She picked up the plain white bonnet she was making and began to sew.

She felt as if she had made a thousand plain white bonnets and a thousand homespun dresses, all gray, all alike. She wished rebelliously she could make a pink bonnet with rosebuds for her pretty little sister. She wished that she could make a red or blue velvet dress.

Mr. Griscom came in to tend the fire for the night. "I thought thee was already in bed," he said. "Thy mother and thy sisters are probably asleep. Surely the sewing can wait."

"Father, I just found out that Webster's take women as apprentices. I know how to do needle-work. I'd like so much to learn upholstering."

"I have always taken care of all my girls, and none of them have had to work away from home," Mr. Griscom said decidedly. "Thee can help thy mother and if thee likes, do a little sewing for other people until thee is married."

"But Father, there are so many girls here to help Mother," Betsy exclaimed. "If I could be apprenticed, I could earn some money to help the family before long."

"Betsy, Betsy, where does thee get all these ideas?" her father asked. "Thy sisters seem to be contented at home."

"Then may I go?" asked Betsy eagerly.

"Webster's might not take thee for an apprentice, Betsy, even if I said thee could go," said Mr. Griscom, smiling.

"But may I go if they will teach me the work?" Betsy asked eagerly.

"I must think the matter over and then talk to thy mother," said Mr. Griscom. "Go to bed now, and we will talk about it some other time."

"Oh, Father, I thank thee so much," Betsy exclaimed. "I can still make clothes for the family and piece quilts, and do many other things. I'll help Mother all I can."

Betsy now had a number of young brothers and sisters. The house was crowded, and Betsy knew that her father sometimes found it difficult to provide for his large family.

Although Betsy already was a competent seamstress, she was excited at the thought of learning another skill. She liked the idea of meeting new people and of working with John, too.

Although Mrs. Griscom demurred at first, she finally gave her consent to Betsy's working away from home. The details were arranged, and Betsy started on this new adventure with great enthusiasm. Because of her skill in needlework she became a valuable employee in a short time.

These were turbulent times. The colonists resisted more and more the demands of the British. The possibility of war was frequently discussed. Clashes on the streets between the redcoats, as the British soldiers were called, and the townspeople became every-day events.

Talk of liberty for the colonies was rampant at the shop. At first this was bewildering to Betsy. The desire of the colonies for independence was seldom discussed by the Griscoms. She became more and more interested in the affairs of the colonies. She listened to what John and other people said about the wrongs the colonies suffered. She formed her own opinions.

Usually John Ross walked most of the way home with Betsy. Just before they reached her house, he would leave her to go toward Christ Church, where his father was a rector. They found many things to talk about.

They often discussed the growing desire of the colonies to be free. John was an enthusiastic patriot, and Betsy began to agree more and more with his views. She was troubled, however, because her parents did not share her opinions.

"My father and mother are Tories—loyal to the king," she told him. "You know the Friends do not believe in war. They think the differences can be worked out. George and some of my sisters, though, feel as I do."

"All families seem to be divided," John said. "My Uncle John is loyal to the king. He's an attorney general of the colony under the royal governor. My Uncle George, however, sympathizes with the colonists who want to be free."

Even thoughts of war could not quell the high spirits of these young people. They did their work quickly and competently. They were enthusiastic patriots who were liked by their employers and by the other workers in the shop.

John Ross had served most of his apprenticeship. He dreamed more and more of being in his own upholstery shop. But now he dreamed of having Betsy share that shop with him.

Betsy's dreams were like John's. She wanted to share his life. If he went to war—he often spoke of enlisting in the colonial militia—she could take care of the shop until he returned.

A Famous Story

MANY years later Ruth and Jim Wills were walking along Arch Street in Philadelphia. They had already visited Carpenter's Hall and a number of other places of historical interest.

At Independence Hall they had stood looking at the Liberty Bell for a long time. They had been awed by being in the place where the Declaration of Independence had been adopted and George Washington had been voted commander-in-chief of the American armies.

They had started out early because there were many places they wanted to see. They planned to visit the Betsy Ross house next.

They crossed the street and stood for a few minutes looking at the two-story house with the little attic. Then they opened the door and went into the front room.

"Good morning." A woman came toward them. "I'm Mrs. Stewart," she said. "Won't you come in? You're our first visitors today. I unlocked the door just a few minutes ago."

"We're Ruth and Jim Wills," Ruth said. "We're sight-seeing in Philadelphia. Have we come before the house is open?"

"Oh, no." Mrs. Stewart smiled at them. "But it's nice you've come early. This is our busy season and sometimes this room gets very crowded. You see, over 150,000 people visit this house every year. Some days we have so many visitors there's scarcely room for everyone."

Jim looked around the little room. "Has the house always been just like this," he asked, "ever since Betsy Ross lived here?"

Mrs. Stewart shook her head. "No," she said, "other people lived in the house after Betsy Ross died. Then in 1898 many important people from all over the United States organized the American Flag House and Betsy Ross Memorial. They bought the house for a historical landmark.

"In 1937," Mrs. Stewart went on, "the house was restored to its original condition by Mr. Atwater Kent. Now the people of Philadelphia are very proud of it. They think it is fortunate that this house of hers has been preserved."

Ruth smiled. "I can't remember when I first heard that Betsy Ross made the first flag," she said. "It seems to me I've known that story as long as I've known my own name. But I haven't any idea how she happened to make it. Was she a flagmaker? Had she made any flags before she made the Stars and Stripes?"

Mrs. Stewart shook her head. "She said she never had made a flag."

"Then how did she happen to make it?" Ruth asked. "Would they ask someone who had never made a flag to make such an important one?"

"Well, you see," Mrs. Stewart began, "as Betsy Griscom she had made quite a name for herself for fine sewing. Even when she was in school she won many honors at exhibits and at the High Street fairs. She was often asked to make designs for quilts, and was known for her artistic ability.

"When John Ross married Betsy," Mrs. Stewart continued, "both of them were working as apprentices in a leading upholstery shop in the city. After they were married, they opened their own shop here in this room."

"I should think it was a poor time to start a business of that kind," said Jim.

"Business was brisk from the very start," said Mrs. Stewart. "It is easy to believe that Betsy Ross, well known for her skill in sewing, might have been chosen to make the first flag.

"But that isn't all," Mrs. Stewart added. "There's another reason why she might have been chosen. Betsy's husband John Ross had an uncle named Colonel George Ross. He was a very close friend of General George Washington and a member of his staff. Colonel Ross later signed the Declaration of Independence."

At that moment the door opened and a dignified, gray-haired lady came in.

"Oh, how nice!" Mrs. Stewart hurried to meet her. Then, turning to Ruth and Jim, she said, "This will be a very pleasant surprise for you. I want you to meet Miss Edna Randolph Worrell, a great-great-grandneice of Betsy Ross.

"Miss Worrell, this is Ruth and Jim Wills. I was just going to tell them the story that is told of the making of the first flag. I know it would mean much more if you would tell it to them."

"I've told it many times," Miss Worrell said, smiling, "but I never tire of telling it."

"We'd like very much to hear it," Ruth said.

"When I was a little girl, Mrs. Susan Turner, my grandmother, used to tell us this story over and over about her Aunt Betsy," said Miss Worrel. "Now I'm the family storyteller.

"Let's imagine for a few minutes that we are living in Philadelphia almost two hundred years ago, in June 1776. General Washington had come to Philadelphia to consult with members of congress. He needed men and supplies to fight the British. He was looking for ways to unite the colonies that were still divided.

"Most of the states and many of the ships were using their own emblems. General Washington felt that it was very important to have a national standard for the army and the navy. He discussed this new flag with Mr. Robert Morris and Colonel George Ross. He had drawn a design and wanted to have a flag made. Is it not probable that Colonel Ross would suggest his own niece?

"Early one morning Mrs. Betsy Ross was getting her shop ready for another busy day. She must have dusted the furniture and swept the hearth. Then she answered a knock on the door.

"Standing there were Colonel George Ross, her husband's uncle, Mr. Robert Morris, one of the richest men in Pennsylvania, and General George Washington. She invited them inside.

"General Washington showed her a sketch of the flag. He asked her if she could make one in the same design out of bunting.

"Betsy Ross said she didn't know, but she would try. The design had six white stripes and seven red ones. In the upper left-hand corner was a blue field with a cluster of thirteen stars. She knew the thirteen stars and stripes must be for the thirteen colonies.

"Then she noticed that the stars had six points. 'I think it is a beautiful design,' she said, 'but I believe five-pointed stars would look better.'

"Betsy folded a small piece of cloth several times and cut it once with her scissors. Then, unfolding it, she showed the men a perfect five-pointed star. They agreed to the change."

"She must have been a very busy person," said Ruth, fascinated by the story.

"Indeed she must have been," said Miss Worrell. "Her young husband, who had joined the militia, had been killed in January when ammunition in a storehouse he was guarding exploded. Betsy, who was only twenty-four, was carrying on the business alone.

"We know Betsy Ross made many flags after that," Miss Worrell went on. "There are records of money paid to her for flags, and bills for bunting made out in her own hand.

"Many people and many organizations have honored her through the years, and now we have this." Miss Worrell picked up a postage stamp and showed it to Ruth and Jim.

"Betsy Ross was born January 1, 1752," said she. "Congress directed the Post Office Department to issue a stamp on January 1, 1952, to honor the two-hundredth anniversary of her birth.

"See, it shows her displaying the new flag to General Washington, Robert Morris, and George Ross. They are sitting here in this house. The design was taken from a painting by Charles H. Weisberger, one of the founders and first secretary of the Memorial Association."

Ruth and Jim looked around the room. The people who had created the first emblem of a great country seemed very near.

"Philadelphia is like a great history book," Ruth said. "I'm so glad we came here."

"We thank you for telling us this story, Miss Worrell," Jim said. "You've made history seem very real to us. I see a group of other people are arriving. We saw Independence Hall and the Liberty Bell yesterday—"

Miss Worrell smiled. "Betsy and the Liberty Bell were twins," she said. "They both arrived in the same year. And Betsy's father, Samuel Griscom, helped build the belfry of Independence Hall. They were called the State House and the State House Bell when she was a little girl, but she was right here in Philadelphia when they got their new names. She was a part of our early history in many different ways."

Ruth and Jim knew they weren't saying goodby to Betsy Ross when they left. They would think of her whenever they saw their country's flag.